HANG TOUGH, PAUL MATHER

ALFRED SLOTE

AN AVON CAMELOT BOOK

AVON BOOKS
A division of
The Hearst Corporation
959 Eighth Avenue
New York, New York 10019

First Camelot Printing, March, 1975.

Printed in the U.S.A.

10 9 8 7 6 5 4 3

To Richard L. Prager, M.D.

ALFRED SLOTE is well known for his sports fiction, and more recently, his science fiction. He has written many books for adults and children. He now lives with his wife, Henrietta, in Ann Arbor, Michigan, where he plays squash and writes. He has three grown children.

Contents

HANG TOUGH, PAUL MATHER

1 THE TAPE RECORDER

ONE THING Tom Kinsella could do that none of my other doctors could do was juggle. I found that out one day when he came into my room and spotted the three autographed baseballs.

"Now you've got three of them," he said.

"That's right," I said.

"Who's this one from?"

"The team I used to play with in Texas."

"And this one?"

"The team I used to play with in California."

"And this has got to be the local yokels—Arborville. Right?"

I had to smile at his description of them as "local yokels." He was an Arborville boy himself once . . . a long time ago. I guess you always knock what you like best.

"That's right," I said.

He picked up the three balls, making them look small just by holding them in one hand. "I suppose you know what three balls are good for?"

"What?"

"Juggling."

And darned if he didn't start juggling, right then and there in my hospital room. And him a doctor! I tried not to laugh. Laughing hurt inside. But to think we had traveled more than halfway across the country in order for me to be this guy's patient. In California, they said he was a great doctor. Boy, if they only knew how he practiced medicine!

Finally he caught all three balls in one hand, and there he was, just the way he'd begun.

"How'd you learn to juggle, Tom?"

He put the balls back in the glass ashtray. "Someone taught me. One of these days I'll teach you."

"When?"

"Maybe tomorrow."

"Great."

But Tom Kinsella didn't teach me tomorrow because tomorrow I wasn't feeling so good. He promised the day after, but the day after wasn't any better. Then Dad took the balls out of my room. He said he wanted to show them to the nurses and orderlies at the central desk, but I knew why he did it. Tom Kinsella was annoyed, too. He said he'd get those balls back, but meanwhile he brought me something else. A tape recorder.

"Ever see one of these things before, sport?"

"In stores."

"They're real easy to work. All you do is flip this switch, push in the 'record' button, and start talking."

"Start talking about what?"

"About how you hit two home runs in one inning back in Texas."

"How'd you know about that?"

"Your dad. They must have had terrible pitching in Texas. This is the mike. You just hold it up and talk into it. Maybe talk about the perfect game you pitched in California against the team from Santa Barbara. Your dad didn't tell me about that one, sport. I saw the newspaper clipping on that one. Your little brother showed it to me."

I got a Kleenex and blew my nose. "I don't feel like talking into machines, Tom."

He rubbed my head. "Maybe you will later. Besides, you don't have to talk only about your victories. Tell about your defeats. You did lose once in a while, didn't you?"

This time I did laugh. "Yes, I lost. But that was here in Arborville, and you already know about that one. It got me back in the hospital."

"Other people don't know, sport. Tell them about it. Tell them about Arborville. Tell them about me."

It's hard to argue with a doctor. I didn't say no; I didn't say yes, but one night when I was having a hard time sleeping, I turned on the lamp, flipped the "On" switch on the tape recorder, pushed the "Record" button, picked up the microphone, and began talking about Arborville. Arborville was the last stop on a long line, but it was a good stop. It's easier to talk about happy things than unhappy things, so that's why I'm telling you about Arborville.

2 ARRIVAL IN ARBORVILLE

COMING INTO ARBORVILLE was like coming into any other small city in the United States. You went past drive-in movies, drive-in restaurants, drive-in car washes, drive-in banks which had whirling signs on them that gave you the time on one side and the temperature on the other. I can still remember the temperature that day in June when we drove in—it was seventy-one degrees, and I remember thinking that it was the exact same temperature when we left Palo Alto four days before.

Larry said: "This looks just like Palo Alto."

"It looks like Austin, too," I said.

"All towns look alike on the outskirts," Dad said. "You have to get inside them, into the old parts, to see where they're different."

"Hmm," Mom said, which she always said when she thought Dad was making a pronouncement—like a professor. Which he was. Mom never liked him teaching after class.

"Anyway," Larry said, "I hope this place is as good as Palo Alto."

Larry is my kid brother. He's also known as the Pest or the Punk depending on how I feel on a certain day. He's ten years old, and I have to admit that for a punk he's pretty good at handling a basketball. Maybe you have to be a punk to be good at hot dog games like basketball. He's too small to really shoot well, but he can dribble the pants off you. And he's always practicing. He dribbles balls all over the house, upstairs, downstairs, in the basement. He can watch a TV show and practice dribbling between his legs. And he can dribble with his left hand as well as he can with his right. The world begins and ends with basketball for the Punk and his biggest concern about our new house in Arborville was whether or not there would be a backboard on the garage.

I'd been telling him ever since California that the house didn't even have a garage, that Arborville was a hockey town in winter, and he'd have to quit sports for good.

Mom told me not to tease him and Dad said the house did, too, have a garage as I perfectly well knew, but he couldn't remember if there had been a backboard up or not. Certainly, if there wasn't one, he'd try to get permission from the owners to put one up.

"But they've left town, Dad," I reminded him, "so if there isn't one up, we can't put one up."

"Paul," Mom warned me.

"I'll get permission from the trust company," Dad said

quietly, but I knew he was getting angry. "They're the ones renting the house for the Boyles."

"I gotta have a backboard," the Pest said. "You said I'd have a backboard when we left California."

"There will be a backboard for you, Larry," Dad said. "There will be a backboard if I have to rent a gym for you."

And that quieted the Punk down for a while. But after another hundred miles or so, he'd start up again. The truth was, the Punk hadn't wanted to leave California. He was too young to enjoy Texas, but he really came of sporting age in California; he had good friends, he was known as a hotshot basketball player and a pretty good shortstop, and he didn't want to go. He blamed me for making everyone leave and so he was doubly mad when I teased him about no backboard in Arborville.

And now, twenty-five hundred miles and four days later, as we were entering Arborville, the Punk was deciding it wasn't his kind of place.

"It looks junky," he said, as we drove by some more motels and car washes.

"So did Palo Alto," I said.

"Both of you stop living in the past," Dad said. "This is Arborville."

As if to punctuate his words, a sign appeared on the right that said:

```
┌─────────────────────────────────────────┐
│        ARBORVILLE CITY LIMITS           │
│                                         │
│              WELCOME                    │
│                                         │
│            DRIVE SLOWLY                 │
│                                         │
│      HOME OF A GREAT UNIVERSITY         │
└─────────────────────────────────────────┘
```

"What's so great about this university?" the Punk asked.

"It's great 'cause it's here," I said.

"Ssh, both of you," Mom said. "Look, it's changing. Why, it's a lovely town."

The fact was, after that sign the town began to change, and for the better. There were big trees on the sides of the avenue, and big old white and brick houses, and wide sweeping lawns.

"Hey, this isn't all bad," Larry said.

"I'm sure they're fraternity houses," Dad said.

"Do we live near here, Frank?" Mom asked.

"Not far, I think. Do you remember, Paul?"

"I think it's around here somewhere."

Dad and I had come out here in February to visit the hospital and Dr. Kinsella and rent a house but I could barely remember anything at all.

"Maybe there's a backboard at the school," the Punk said. "How far do we live from our school?"

"Not far."

"How far from a park?"

"Not far."

"Dad, that's all you keep saying. 'Not far.' "

Dad laughed. I could feel for him. It was either laugh or blow your stack.

But I could feel for the Punk too. Because that's how it is at the end of a long trip. Last night in Iowa, today in Michigan, and he could not wait. He thought every house was his house (especially the ones with backboards) and so far none of them had been.

"I think we're coming into our neighborhood now," Dad said. "What do you think, Paul?"

"It looks familiar."

All I could remember from that quick trip in February was a lot of winding streets and a lot of trees.

Dad made a left turn off the wide avenue we'd come in on, and then another left, then a right, and a left. It was a regular fox trail. I wondered how we'd ever learn to find our way around here. Everything was woods and houses set far back. Then suddenly we were in a narrow winding line that was very familiar. Dad made an abrupt turn into a driveway and we were there.

"Here we are," he said.

"There's no backboard," Larry said.

"Shut up," I said.

"It's lovely, Frank," Mom said, and we all knew she was disappointed. It was a small house. Only two bedrooms. In Palo Alto we had four bedrooms, a study, a two-car garage, and a swimming pool, too. This was a nice little house in the woods.

"It's small," Dad said, "but it's nice inside."

Larry was first out of the car. He usually is. He studied the garage. He was determined not to be downcast.

"Hey, it's got the right kind of roof, anyway."

"We'll get permission from the trust company," Dad said, "and we'll put one up right away. That will be first on the agenda."

Dad was a softy.

"And look at all those trees, Frank. We're really in the woods, aren't we?"

"A lot of leaves to rake," Dad said, smiling.

The Punk dribbled an imaginary ball and threw it up to an imaginary hoop. "It's OK," he announced, "we can go one on one here pretty good."

He was right about that. It was a small driveway, but wide and level, so you didn't have to go uphill like you do on driveways that are well graded. It was a good basketball house, but not very good for baseball. There were too many trees to throw a ball around, let alone hit one. And you couldn't play in the lane, it was too narrow and winding.

I looked at Dad as he was searching his pocket for the house key, and I wondered if he had rented us a house with a yard full of trees on purpose, so I wouldn't be tempted to pitch a baseball.

No, it was more likely he'd rented it because it was cheap. University teaching jobs weren't as easy to get as when we moved from Texas to California, and this time Dad had had to accept a job with less pay. Anyway, it wasn't supposed to make any difference to me. I wasn't supposed to play ball until I had my new doctor's permission.

Dad opened the door. "Come on, let's look inside."

I left Larry working on his jump shot which always

worked as long as he didn't use a real ball, and followed Mom and Dad inside.

"This is a lovely home, Frank. And what a beautiful bookcase. Just look at that dining room table! And look here, a modern kitchen, and here's a half bath. This must be the door to the basement. . . . Here's the back door, and a nice big back hallway, and here are the stairs to the upstairs. Come on, Paul, let's look at your and Larry's room."

The Punk and I were going to share a room for the first time in years.

"Where is Larry, Paul?" Dad asked.

"Still outside."

"You'd better get him in. I don't know what the neighbors will think. New people move in and a ten-year-old child is jumping up and down with an imaginary ball in his hand."

"They'll think he's crazy, which he is."

I went outside expecting to see the Punk doing just what Dad had described. To my surprise, Larry was standing on the sidewalk talking with three kids in baseball uniforms. As I opened the door I heard the Punk saying: "My brother was the best Little League pitcher in northern California last year. He pitched three no-hitters."

I groaned.

Larry heard me. He turned. "Hey, Paul, these guys are your age. They live around here."

"Dad wants you inside."

"OK, but come here first."

I knew it would be a mistake to go over there. I'd been sent to get Larry inside, not to meet a bunch of baseball players. If I hadn't gone it might have made all the difference in the world, though Dr. Kinsella keeps telling me no.

"Maybe you just got back in here a little sooner, sport," he says. "But baseball didn't put you back here. Lots of little white blood cells did."

That's what Tom Kinsella says. But the fact was, I did go over to meet those guys, and everything that happened to me in my very short season came out of that meeting.

3 PITCH IN A WINDING LANE

IN CALIFORNIA we didn't have teams with names like Wilson Dairy or Baer Machine or Ace Appliance. We were Little League teams and we had sponsors but we had names like the White Sox or the Angels or the Yankees. And we had farm teams that had real farm team names.

I could see right away that here in Michigan things were different. The three kids talking to the Punk had WILSON DAIRY lettered across their shirts. But once you got past that—and frankly, it was pretty hard getting past that—things were the same. I mean, these kids were looking me over just the way I'd been looked over in California when we'd arrived from Texas. I was a new kid in town; was I a ball player? If so, could I help the team? What was my position? Could I hit?

What I couldn't tell them was that I probably shouldn't be playing ball at all. At least not until I got my new doctor's permission. It was plain dumb of me even to come out to talk with them and even to look at a baseball. One thing I learned from being sick was that if you stayed away long enough from something you loved—like baseball—you didn't miss it so much. You forgot how good it was.

The Punk was a hot dog—for himself as well as for everybody else in the family. And one thing about being a hot dog is, you never think ahead. You never see consequences.

"Paul," Larry said, "these guys need a pitcher."

"Are you a pitcher?" a kid asked me. He looked to be the leader. Sandy-haired, pug-nosed, freckled, and chewing gum. He had a funny croaky kind of voice.

"I used to pitch," I told him.

"Who for?" the kid asked.

"A team in California."

"He pitched three no-hitters last year," the Pest spoke up again. "And he pitched a perfect game against Santa Barbara in the state tournament."

"Gee, he must be good," a kid with a catcher's mitt said.

"Maybe. Maybe not," the leader said, and spat. "California ain't Michigan, not by a long shot. What's your name, kid?"

"Paul Mather."

"I'm Monk Lawler."

"His real name is John," said the kid with the catcher's mitt. "Only no one calls him John."

"Shut up, Tip." Monk spat again into the lane. His spit flew about ten feet. A ball player, I thought. It was one sure way you could tell a ball player.

"How old are you?" Monk asked me.

"He's twelve," Larry put in, "same as you guys."

God, was my kid brother dumb. He was so very, very dumb.

"What grade are you in?"

"He's in sixth," Larry said, beaming.

"What's the matter? Can't he talk for himself?"

Larry blushed.

Monk turned back to me. "Can you pitch?"

My heart gave a thump. *Don't be a fool,* a little voice inside me said. *Get back inside the house.*

"I used to pitch."

With a quick motion, Monk flipped a baseball at me. I caught it and for just a second I was tempted to squeeze it, grip it, get the feel of it, but the smarter part of me resisted. I flipped it back at him.

"I *used* to pitch."

"What's that mean?"

"It means I don't pitch anymore."

"Why not?"

I turned to Larry. "Mom and Dad want you inside."

Larry looked embarrassed. Like he had started something he couldn't finish.

"Hold on, kid," Monk said. "How come you don't pitch anymore."

"I was sick."

"What'd you have?" Tip asked.

"Nothing catching," I said. "C'mon, Larry."

"Was your arm sick too?" Monk asked.

"No."

"So let's see you pitch."

This time he held the ball out to me. This time it wasn't an order. It was an invitation and a challenge.

Don't take it, the voice inside me said.

"Hey, fella," the third kid said, smiling, "Michigan balls don't bite."

"Besides," Monk said, "if you really were pitching all them no-hitters in California like your brother said, you got to show us what a great pitcher looks like."

They weren't challenging me anymore, they were laughing at me. Now it was a matter of pride. I reached over and took the baseball from Monk.

"Paul, we better go in," Larry said uneasily.

"Now *he's* starting," Monk said.

"I think it's a comedy act," the third kid said.

I hardly heard them laughing at us, the baseball felt so good in my hand. It was scuffed up, too, the kind you like to throw, the kind you can do things with. I throw my curve fingers against the seam. I throw my fast ball with the seam. I moved my fingers around the ball. They belonged there. The ball belonged in my hand. I'd forgotten what it felt like. Baseball was my game, pitching was my life. I was born to pitch.

Monk Lawler stepped into the lane. "C'mon," he said, "let's see what you've got."

"Paul," the Punk said, "you better not."

"Hey, you gonna throw or pose?" Monk Lawler asked. He was waiting for me. "Let's go."

I stepped into the lane. It was as simple and as dumb as that.

Monk started to back up. I stopped him.

"Hold it there. I haven't thrown since last August. Stay close for a while."

"Well, he talks like a pitcher, doesn't he, Abels?" Tip said.

"So do lots of guys," Abels, the third kid, said. "Monk, you better hurry up, we got a game in a little while."

"Hey," Tip said, "he don't look so great."

I was lobbing them to Monk from a short distance. He lobbed them back to me. I didn't have a glove on. No one offered me a glove. I jerked my hands back as I caught the ball to take some of the sting off. My hands were soft, but my fingers were strong. So far, my arm felt fine.

"OK, back up another ten feet," I ordered Monk.

He backed up.

"He sure doesn't rush things," Abels said.

"You're about softball distance now," Tip said to me.

"Don't worry about it," I said. I threw a half dozen more easy ones and it still felt good. I backed Monk up till he was Little League pitching distance away—forty-five feet.

"Stop there."

"Well, he knows the pitching distance," Tip said approvingly.

"It still doesn't make him a pitcher," Abels said. "It might make him an umpire, though."

I threw easily at regulation distance and ignored the wisecracks. Monk wasn't mouthing off and neither was my kid brother Larry. He was standing there looking very uneasy. Well, he'd started it and I was going to finish it.

"OK, I'm ready."

"Paul, don't throw hard," Larry said.

I ignored him. "You better borrow that catcher's mitt, Monk," I said.

"Here, Monk," Tip said, holding up the mitt.

"Forget it," Monk growled, and went down in a squat with his glove. A Michigan toughie, I thought, and grinned.

"Straight in," I said.

"Paul," Larry warned.

I pumped, rocked, and fired my next-to-fast one. Monk caught it and was bowled over backward. He got up slowly, and then even more slowly he took his hand out of his glove and examined it.

"You OK?" I asked.

He looked at me. "Yeah. Maybe."

The other two Dairy kids were staring at me, but Larry, my dumb jerk of a brother, was grinning. "I told you he could throw, and that's not even his fast one. He—"

"Shut up, Pest." I looked down at Monk. "You set?"

"Nope," Monk said. He flipped his glove at Tip. "Gimme your mitt, Tip."

Tip caught Monk's glove and tossed Monk his big catcher's mitt. "Let me catch him, Monk."

"Not yet," Monk said, and went down into his squat. "What're you gonna throw?"

"This time I'll throw my fast ball."

"What was that other pitch?"

"That was my off-speed pitch."

"Oh. That's nice. OK, bub, let her fly."

I pumped, rocked, and let her fly. The ball smacked into his mitt and Monk was moved backward, but he didn't fall down. He had braced himself this time.

"Nice," he muttered, grimacing. "Very nice. Tip, you got a sponge?"

"Nope," Tip said, grinning, "I don't need a sponge for you."

"Thanks." Monk turned to me. "Throw something else, will you?"

Tip and Abels laughed. Larry was smiling proudly.

"Curve going that way," I said, pointing to the left.

"I'm with you," Monk grunted.

But he wasn't. It broke too sharply for him, got by him, and rolled all the way up to the corner.

"Holy cow," Abels said.

"Wait till Jim Anderson sees him."

"Guys in our league don't even throw curves yet."

Monk came back with the ball. He held it. "I guess I've seen enough."

"No, you haven't," I said.

I was bitten. It had been a long time since I had pitched, and I wasn't going to stop now. I hadn't wanted it to start up again, but now that it was started, I wanted it to go on and on and on.

"Paul," Larry said, nervously, "maybe you better—"

"Curve going the other way," I said to Monk and fired off my version of a slider. It wasn't too good, but it moved a little.

After that I fired my next-to-fast ball, then a change of pace, and then I broke off some more curves. I was beginning to feel in the groove. I was sweating. Sweat lubricates a pitcher. It gets all his moving parts working together. I was beginning to get a rhythm. It was like I hadn't taken a year's break at all. This was what it was all about. This was what you lived for and why you lived.

"Fast one," I said.

"Change-up.

"Curve that way.

"Slider, I hope.

"Sinker, maybe."

"Oops, sorry. It got away."

"Fast ball."

"Don't throw it. My hand hurts."

"Change-up, then."

"Thanks, California."

I fired some fifteen pitches and on the last one I cut loose again. Monk caught it and stood up.

"That will do it," he announced, examining his hand, which was red. "That will jolly well do it." He blew on his hand and flexed his fingers. "If I blow the game today, it's your fault, bub. How about coming over to the park with us and meeting our coach?"

For a second I was going to do it. I was actually going to leave with them to meet their coach. Larry couldn't have stopped me, and I could not have stopped myself. The only one who could have stopped me . . . did.

"Paul," my father's quiet voice called from the front steps of the house, "could you and Larry come in now?"

He wasn't angry, and yet I had the feeling he'd been standing there for some time watching.

"I got to go," I said. "C'mon, Larry."

"Sampson Park's just two blocks up there."

"Come over and watch us play."

"Jim Anderson, our coach, will want to meet you."

"None of our guys can pitch half as good as you."

"We could really use you, Paul."

"We're not gonna make the playoffs without a pitcher like you."

"Hey, wait up, Paul. We—"

Tip and Abels were doing all the talking. Monk Lawler was silent. He was trying to figure out what was wrong. The way my father stood there, waiting for me to come in, he knew that something was wrong.

4 BALL PARK DETOUR

INSIDE, the Punk was sitting on the couch trying hard not to cry. Mom had probably yelled at him, wanting to know why he hadn't stopped me. I wondered if Larry had had the guts to tell her he was the one who'd got me involved with those guys in the first place.

Dad came in behind me. "Sit down, Paul," he said quietly.

"I know, Dad."

"What do you know, Paul?"

"That I'm not supposed to be pitching a baseball or do anything until I see Dr. Kinsella."

"Why did you do it, then?"

I felt rather than saw Larry look at me. I shrugged. "Because I wanted to."

Larry breathed out.

But it was the truth, too. I wasn't saving him. He had nothing to do with my decision to accept that baseball from Monk and pitch in the lane. No one talks people into doing things they really want to do. I knew that. And Dad knew that too.

"Paul," Dad said, "wasn't that an unreasonable thing to do?"

My dad's a geology professor. He lives the life of reason and expects everyone else to.

"Yes," I said, and knew I couldn't explain to him that I'd been reasonable for almost a year and avoided the touch of a baseball. But now I'd touched it, thrown it, and now baseball was back in my blood right along with my rotten disease. But Dad, who wasn't an athlete, couldn't be expected to know that. Still, I thought, he hadn't stopped me either. He must have been watching for a while, too. He must have understood something, too.

"Dad, I'll try not to do it again."

Dad nodded. "All right, you better go upstairs and wash up. You too, Larry. We're going out for supper."

The Punk took off like a shot, taking the stairs two at a time. I went up slowly. I knew they would be watching me. I heard Mom say: "Is that all you're going to say to him, Frank?"

"Yes," Dad said, and I blessed him silently.

"Hey, Paul," Larry said, "this is our room."

I walked into a small bedroom that had bunk beds in it and a desk. Over the desk was a framed baseball picture. In color. A bunch of kids and an adult coach.

"I guess whoever lives in this room is a baseball player," I said.

"His kid brother's probably a good one too," the Punk said.

"Who says he's got a kid brother?"

"Aw, Paul, why would they have bunk beds if he didn't have a kid brother?"

"Dummy, he had the bunk bed because he wanted a friend to sleep over."

Larry got mad. "I bet you anything he's got a brother and I bet the brother is a good ball player. I bet he's a great basketball player."

"I bet you're full of it," I said, laughing.

"I don't care anyway," Larry said. He dove into the lower bunk. "Hey, can I have the bottom?"

"Sure. If I wet my bed, just duck."

"You can have the bottom if you want it."

"No, thanks. I'd rather look at the ceiling than your rear end."

The Punk giggled. It wasn't hard to make him giggle.

"Boys," Mom called up the stairs, "are you getting washed up?"

"We're almost done, Mom," Larry said, and ran into the bathroom. I followed him in. It was a nice big bathroom with a view of a back yard that also had a lot of trees in it.

"Boy, we're living in a real forest," the Punk said.

"C'mon, wash up."

He washed up and then I washed up but neither of us did too well. It's hard to wash off twenty-five hundred miles just like that.

"Mom, which are our towels?" Larry called out.

"You're blue and Paul's red."

"These people were nice to leave towels for us," Larry said.

"We left towels for the people moving into our house."

"I'd like to meet the kids who live here."

"Maybe we will."

"No way," the Punk said. "We're going back to California in July. That Dr. Kinsella is going to fix you up, Paul, and then we're going back home."

It was all nice and tidy in his ten-year-old mind. I never really knew what the Punk knew about my disease; we never discussed it much. Right now he knew I was holding my own and that was good enough for us both.

By the time Larry and I had gone downstairs, Dad had brought in all the luggage.

"I could have helped you with that," I said.

"There wasn't much," Dad said, with both of us looking at a living room full of suitcases.

"Let's go eat now," Mom said. "We have a lot of work to do when we get back. I want to rearrange the furniture."

"What's wrong with the way it is now?" Larry asked.

"I don't like it. That's what's wrong. Frank, where will we eat?"

"I saw a pizza place coming in," Larry said.

"Don't you ever get tired of pizzas?" Dad asked, holding the door open for us.

"Never."

I hung back a little so I could walk to the car with Dad.

"I'm going to help you unpack when we get back," I said to him quietly.

"Let's eat first," Dad said. "We can discuss it later."

Which only meant he was going to continue to treat me carefully. It was frustrating.

In the car the usual argument started about where we were going to eat. Larry was still pushing for his pizza place. Mom and Dad wanted a real restaurant, someplace with tablecloths. I pointed out that we had a lot of unpacking to do and a restaurant with tablecloths never took less than two hours. That swung the victory to pizzas.

Dad backed the car into the lane. "I'm going to head back to that avenue we came in on," he announced.

"I know how you can get there, Dad," Larry said.

"How's that?" Dad asked, amused because usually Larry had no sense of direction. I looked at the Punk curiously. I knew him well enough to know he was planning something.

"You go two blocks that way and turn to the right."

"Are you sure?" Dad asked.

"Yep," Larry said.

I grinned. I knew what the Punk was planning. I had to hand it to him. He was maneuvering with a straight face.

Dad followed Larry's instructions. Up two blocks, a right turn, and no sooner did we make the right turn than we could hear the noise, and Dad knew he'd been taken.

"Hey, batter, batter . . ."

"No batter in there."

"Pitcher's going up, up, up . . ."

"Wait him out."

"Make him pitch to you."

"No stick."

Dad was torn between being mad and amused and he

solved it by deciding to be amused. "So this is how to go to a pizza place, Larry."

"Aw, Dad," Larry said, "we could just watch for a second."

On our left was the park. Sampson Park. A big park, and there was a parking lot, and to the right of the parking lot a baseball diamond. There was another diamond in the middle of the park, but on this diamond near us and the parking lot, the Wilson Dairy team was playing. They were at bat.

"Let's just see them hit," the Punk said, grinning at me.

Dad looked at Mom. She shrugged. "All right, but I don't know how we're going to find that avenue we came in on."

"No sweat," Larry said. "We can ask someone. Look, they got basketball courts over there."

Dad pulled into a parking place and Larry jumped out almost before the car stopped. "There're two courts," he announced. "There's another one near that building. Hey, that must be the school."

"Isn't it a lovely school?" Mom said. "And so near, too."

"Come on, Paul," Larry said.

I got out of the car.

"Please don't go away from the car, Paul," Mom said. "We're not staying more than a second." She and Dad were staying inside the car.

"Don't worry, Mom," I said.

I took a deep breath. The noises, the shouts, the sight of a baseball game again . . . it felt good. One coach yelling instructions to his batter, the opposing coach moving his left fielder back, the third baseman spitting into his glove, the shortstop yelling at his pitcher, and the pitcher looking lonely on the mound. I could have been back in California or Texas and so, for the first time, Arborville seemed real to me.

"Give it a ride, Cliff baby," a Dairy kid yelled.

The pitch came down, Cliff baby's bat came around, and a high foul was coming over the backstop toward us, bouncing toward the cars. Moving quickly, instinctively, Larry cut in front of the cars, went down on one knee, and grabbed the ball.

All eyes on the diamond had followed the path of the foul ball, and now those eyes had discovered us.

"Hey, it's Paul," Tip, the catcher, called out.

"It's Paul Mather, the kid we were telling you about," the other kid, Abels, said.

"Come on over, Paul," Tip yelled.

"Jim," Abels said, "that's the kid who can throw so hard. He's not on any team yet."

"Paul, c'mere."

"Ball in," the other team's catcher called out. He was anxious to get the old scuffed-up ball back in the game. Smart move. Pitchers hate smooth new balls.

"Ball in," the ump called out to us.

"Wing it in, Paul," Tip yelled.

Larry looked at me. Aware that my folks were watching from the car, I shook my head. "You throw it," I said.

Larry threw it back to the catcher.

"All right, boys," Dad called, "you've seen enough. Let's go now."

We hadn't seen enough. We hadn't seen anything. But Dad was trying to beat the Dairy coach to the punch. Jim Anderson, the Dairy coach, was running toward us.

"Let's go," Dad said, raising his voice, "now!"

But Jim Anderson got to us before we got to the car. It was a race I hadn't wanted to win.

"Excuse me," he puffed, "you're Paul Mather, aren't you?"

I nodded. I didn't dare say anything . . . yet.

"I'm Jim Anderson, coach of Wilson Dairy. Mr. Mather, Mrs. Mather, I'm Jim Anderson."

Dad nodded. Mom didn't even nod. She looked angry.

Jim Anderson ignored the storm signals. "Monk Lawler, my team captain, told me you people have moved to Arborville and that Paul here is quite a pitcher."

On the diamond, a pitch was thrown, wide for a ball. Jim turned to watch. His attention was in two places; he was recruiting and coaching at the same time.

"I'm glad to welcome you to town. The league doesn't let youngsters sign up after the season's started unless they moved in from out of—"

"Paul is not playing baseball this season," Dad said abruptly. "Nice to have met you, Mr. Anderson. Boys, lock your doors."

"I could make all the arrangements," Jim Anderson went on. "Why don't I give you a call tonight after the game. Monk and Tip and Stu Abels say they never saw anyone throw harder in their lives. I'd like to—"

The crack of a bat turned Jim Anderson around. The batter hit a ball through the infield. He made a wide turn at first and ducked back in.

"Way to hit that ball, Cliff," Jim Anderson called out. "I got to get back to my team. We may have a rally going. Nice to have met you, Mr. Mather, Mrs. Mather. I hope to see you soon, Paul."

And off he ran. He looked pretty young.

Dad started the car up and we backed out.

"Well," Mom said furiously, "that was really very wise of you, Larry, to think of embarrassing Paul all over again."

"I wasn't embarrassed, Mom."

"To place temptation in his way again."

"Aw, Mom," Larry said.

"Don't you 'Aw, Mom' me, young man—"

Dad turned left out of the parking lot. I knew he didn't know where he was going. He just wanted to put as much distance between us and the ball game as possible. But I could hear them shouting all the way down the block and just before we turned the corner I could see out of the back window another Dairy kid get a hit and send the guy on first to third. They looked to be a pretty fair team.

"—It was selfish and stupid. Paul's already done one foolish thing today, why does he have to be exposed to this again?"

"What did I do that was so dumb?" I asked angrily. "Throw a baseball? Is that it?"

"Without a doctor's permission."

"That's right. I enjoyed myself without a doctor's permission. Now it seems I'm not even allowed to watch a ball game without a doctor's permission, is that it?"

"You weren't only going to watch that game, Paul." Mom was angry, too. "How long would it have been before they dragged you onto that team? Not very long at all."

"They couldn't drag him on the team," Larry said helpfully. "He doesn't have a uniform."

"Ssh, please, everybody," Dad said. "I think I know how to get back onto that avenue."

He didn't. We drove around in circles, and at one point we were actually headed back toward Sampson Park and the ball game. Finally, in a series of desperate turns, Dad got us onto a wide street that led to the main avenue that led to a pizza place and a supper eaten in silence.

When we got home, Dad told me he'd prefer me to lie down and rest while they unpacked.

"I suppose it wouldn't do me any good to say I wasn't tired," I said.

"No, it wouldn't," Dad said.

You could argue with my mother, but not with my father. I went upstairs and climbed onto the top bunk, wondering if they'd object even to my having the top bunk. I lay there and stared at the cracks in the ceiling and listened to them unpack and move furniture around. I knew why Mom wanted to move furniture. Even if it didn't improve things, it made her feel at home. It made her feel it was *our* place. But moving furniture around doesn't make a house a home, and this house couldn't ever become my home, the way Arborville couldn't ever become my town. What happened at the park, what had just happened downstairs when they wouldn't let me help unpack, convinced me that unless I took matters into my own hands, this year was just going to be a long motel stop while I visited another hospital that had another magic cure for my disease.

I had to do something about it. But what? And how?

I lay there staring at the cracks, as if the future could be read in the cracks of the ceiling of a rented house.

Then the doorbell rang downstairs. It could only be one person, I thought: Jim Anderson, come recruiting.

I jumped down off the top bunk.

5 TIME OUT #1

I'VE GOT TO INTERRUPT my story here. Dr. Tom Kinsella just came into my hospital room.

"How're you doing, sport?" he asked me.

"OK," I said, suspicious on two counts. One, because he was being too casual. And two, because he was carrying a stack of white papers that I knew were lab reports. Whenever he was extra casual with lab reports in hand, I knew there'd be no good news.

I wasn't wrong.

He sat down on the edge of my bed and looked at my tape recorder and the tapes next to the bed. He'd brought me two extra tapes already. "How's the story coming?"

"OK."

"Are you still going to make me the hero?"

"No."

"Why not?"

"Because you haven't cured me. You'll be a hero when you get me out of here."

"Hmmm . . . maybe that's just the kind of challenge a bright young doctor like me needs. Listen, sport—"

Here it comes, I thought. One of these days I'm going to have to tell him I'm stealing his signs. I always know when he's going to throw bad news at me.

"—We're going to have to increase the dosage of your medicine."

I'd seen it coming, and it still hurt.

"Why?"

It was a dumb question, but I was only stalling for time, trying to organize a counterattack. If they had to increase the medicine it meant that what I was taking now wasn't doing the job. The trouble was that the dosage I was taking now was making me sick all the time. It made me nauseous, it gave me a fever, it made my skin burn and then itch. The medicine hurt worse than the disease, and now he wanted to increase the dosage.

"Why can't I get transfusions?"

Transfusions were uncomfortable, but you didn't get them every day and they didn't hurt like the medicine did. In California they had given me transfusions.

Tom smiled. "You liked those transfusions, did you?"

"Don't joke me, Tom."

"I'm not joking you, sport. It's just that it's sometimes hard to explain to a twelve-year-old."

"Why don't you try?"

He nodded. "OK, I'll try. First of all, at this moment you don't need a transfusion. Secondly, the transfusions don't cure. They give us time by giving you the blood cells you may need. But they don't stop what causes the trouble. The drugs might. We're learning a lot about the drugs. We've still got some to learn, but we're getting there."

"Can't you get there experimenting with someone else?"

"We're not experimenting with you, sport. We've already done the experimenting in the labs. We're trying to find your right level of therapy. We're trying to cure you."

"You're trying to cure me with stuff that's making me sick."

"It could make you well, too."

"How can something make you sick and well at the same time?" I was sounding reasonable but being unreasonable, and we both knew it.

He was patient. "Look, sport. I know the stuff is awful. I know it feels awful. I know it makes you itch and want to throw up. Frankly, you couldn't *pay* me to take it—"

I started to laugh. I didn't want to laugh.

"Easy, sport."

"You ought to be on TV, Tom."

"First, I want to make it into those tapes of yours. When do I get in?"

"You're in already."

"Good or bad?"

"Bad."

"OK, just don't ask me for any help with the medical end of things."

"I don't need any help with the medical end of things. I got the medical end right inside me."

"I meant with words, names, vocabulary."

"I don't need any help with that either. I know the words and names and vocabulary. I—" I hesitated, because what I was going to say I'd never said to anyone. "I . . . even know the name of the disease that I've got."

I looked him right in the eye as I said that and he looked back at me. Since I'd been his patient he'd never used the name. No one in California had ever said it to me. My folks hadn't either. But when you live inside hospitals for long periods of time you hear lots of things . . . in halls, in rooms. People often think you're sleeping when you're not.

"Sport," Tom Kinsella said softly, "you're not going to throw me a curve ball without a warning, are you?"

If that wasn't a warning, what did he think it was?

"I'm just telling you, I know what I've got."

"What do you have, sport?" he asked carefully.

"Leukemia."

"I see. And what is that?"

"It's . . . cancer of the blood. And there's no cure for it. There's never going to be a cure for it. I— I—"

My little speech fell apart. I started to cry. Out of nowhere I started to cry. The dumbest thing in the world . . . crying. And the crazy part was, it didn't hurt to cry. Not the way it hurt to laugh.

Tom let me cry. He didn't say a thing. He let me cry like a big old baby. I'd been bottling up that secret for a long time and now it was spilling out all over my face. Finally, he took a handkerchief out of his pocket and handed it to me. I wiped my face and blew my nose and apologized for behaving like an ass.

"Don't apologize, sport," he said. "You've got at least

one fact wrong. Some day there will be a cure for leukemia. Good people all over the world, the best scientists, are working day and night to discover a cure."

"If they don't have a cure for it why do I have to take the rotten medicine?"

"Because it just may work in your case."

"But if a little bit isn't working why would a lot?"

"Sport, that's like asking if a single won't win the game, why hit a home run?"

"You make it sound easy."

"I don't mean to."

"Suppose the home run doesn't work either."

"We'll try something else."

"And wait on the scientists."

"Yes."

"And while I'm waiting everyone else is playing ball and having fun. I could miss the whole baseball season, couldn't I?"

"You could. On the other hand, it could be a few weeks and you'd be out of here."

"And playing ball again?"

"Maybe."

"Say yes!"

"I can't, sport."

"You mean, you won't. You doctors always have to play it safe, don't you?"

Tom didn't answer. He looked at me, and then he stood up and went over to the big glass ashtray that had my three autographed balls in it: the one from Austin, Texas; the one from Palo Alto, California; and the one from Arborville, Michigan. Dad had taken them out of the room but Tom had made him bring them back. He said they cheered the place up, and besides he liked juggling. He hardly got the chance to juggle anymore.

Now he picked up the balls and sure enough started juggling again. He was a crazy doctor. You ask him a question and instead of answering, he starts juggling baseballs.

Suddenly I realized he was saying something. He was talking to me while he was juggling. He talked straight ahead while his eyes followed the up and down movements of the balls.

"I started with tennis balls, Paul. Then I went to oranges, and then one night to prove to my folks how good I was, I went to eggs."

"Eggs?"

"Yes, eggs."

"Did you drop any?"

"The very first time. My older brother started throwing pennies at me while I was juggling, and I dropped one."

The balls he was juggling now were going higher and higher in the sun-filled room. They made large moving shadows on the wall. I couldn't take my eyes off those shadows.

"Did they make you clean up the mess?"

"There wasn't any mess to clean up."

Higher and higher those shadows went.

"How come?"

The shadows vanished. With a quick swoop he caught the balls and kerplunked them back into the ashtray.

"I hard-boiled them first. That's how come."

I started to laugh, but he held up his hand. "Sport, there's a point to it."

"What?"

"A doctor *should* play it safe. That's what medicine is all about."

"I don't care what medicine is all about. I want to play ball again this summer."

Tom smiled. "I've got to go, sport. I've got other patients, believe it or not."

"And I will, too," I shouted after him as he left.

Then I lay back.

It hurt to shout.

6 COACH COMES RECRUITING

BUT NOW I'M BACK in time to before I went to the hospital.

The doorbell was ringing in our new house. I moved fast, expecting it would be Jim Anderson, the coach. My kid brother moved faster. By the time I'd got to the top of the stairs, the Punk had opened the door and he was yelling, "Hey, it's the coach of the Dairy team."

My instinct was to go downstairs and say hello to him and tell him I was ready to play. But I knew it wouldn't work. So I sat down on the top step to see what would happen.

From where I sat I could see the front hall and the door. Jim Anderson was still standing outside the screen door.

Dad came into view. He went up to the screen door but didn't open it to let Jim Anderson in.

"Mr. Mather, I'm Jim Anderson," the coach said. "You may remember, we met a little while ago at the park."

"Oh, yes," Dad said. He remembered Jim perfectly well. He still made no move to open the screen door. It wasn't like Dad.

"I wonder if I could talk with you a moment?" Jim asked.

"Of course," Dad said, and reluctantly he opened the door and let Jim in the house. "You can see, we're still pretty much of a mess here." Dad was pretending that was the reason he hadn't invited Jim in.

"Oh, I know how it is when you move, sir. When I was in the service, my wife and I moved a lot. I know what it feels like. How do you do, ma'am?"

From where I sat I couldn't see Mom but the fact that she didn't answer told me she must be standing there looking grim.

"Larry," Dad said, "would you run out to the car and bring in the orange overnight bag? Here's the key. It's in the trunk."

"Now?"

"Yes, now, please."

"I don't see why you need it now. . . ." Larry went out the door muttering, not understanding they were trying to get rid of him.

"Now, Mr. Anderson," Dad began. "I think I know why you're here. We don't have much time. Paul—"

"One moment, Frank," Mom said. She came to the bottom of the stairs, looked up, and saw me.

"I thought you were resting, Paul."

"I'm not tired."

"Why don't you go lie down anyway."

"I don't want to. I'm coming down."

Ordinarily I do what my parents ask me to do, but this was so foolish I just couldn't. There's a time when you have to assert yourself, and that time was now. I wanted to play baseball again. I could still feel that ball beneath my fingers. I wanted to feel it there again.

"Hello, Mr. Anderson."

"Hello, Paul."

Jim Anderson was standing in the middle of the living room, looking big and uncomfortable. He had his baseball cap in his hand.

"How'd you do tonight?" I asked him.

He shook his head. "We lost 8-7 to a team we beat last year. We're hurting for pitching. Jim Hakken's doing a fine job, but we've got no one after Jim except Monk, and Monk's not really a pitcher. He's an infielder with a good snap throw and the other team usually starts clobbering him after half an inning. And that," he said, turning to my folks, "is why I picked up my ears when Monk, Tip, and Stu Abels told me that a new family had just moved into the neighborhood and they had a twelve-year-old boy who could pitch a baseball pretty good. . . ."

Jim Anderson paused. It had been a big speech for him. Now he wanted someone else to talk. But no one did.

". . . So, well, I . . . uh . . . brought along an entry card. Sort of a permission thing."

He took a crumpled white card out of his pocket.

"It's . . . uh, got to be signed by a parent, and I need a dollar in dues. Once I get the signed card and the buck, Paul's on the team. I've got an extra uniform over at the firehouse where I work. It may be a little wide around the shoulders and short in the legs, but I don't figure it'll hurt Paul's pitching."

He held the entry card toward Dad, but Dad didn't take it.

It was an embarrassing moment. I went over and took the card out of Jim Anderson's outstretched hand.

"Paul," Mom said, "what are you going to do with that?"

"Look at it."

Dad cleared his throat. "It was very thoughtful of you to stop by like this, Mr. Anderson."

"Jim, sir. Everyone calls me Jim. Kids and all."

"Jim, then. I appreciate it. And I know Paul appreciates it very much. But the fact is, Paul's been quite ill this past year and he won't be able to play baseball until we get his new doctor's permission."

"Oh . . . I see," Jim Anderson said, though it was obvious he didn't see at all. He looked me over to see if he could spot what was wrong with me but he couldn't find anything. I watched him trying to figure it out. Then he tried a different tack.

"Paul played in California, didn't he?"

"Yes," Dad said.

"They might have had a lot more pressure on kids than we have here. We're not all that organized. We—"

He had decided I might be emotionally ill. Even Dad had to smile at that.

"No, I'm afraid it's not that, Mr. Anderson. Paul's used to pressure. I daresay as a pitcher he thrived on it, which was what made him so effective. No, I'm sorry to say it's more serious than that and something I don't want to go into right now."

51

At that moment the door opened and the Punk came back with the orange overnight bag and Dad's car keys.

"That trunk is hard to open," he said. He dropped the bag on the floor and gave Dad the car keys. "Well, are you gonna let Paul play for the Dairy team? They sure need him."

There was one thing about the Punk: he didn't beat around the bush.

"Why don't you go upstairs and explore your room?" Mom said.

"Huh?"

"Look over your room."

"Paul and I already looked it over. What about it? You gonna let him play?"

"Paul won't be playing anything until he's seen Dr. Kinsella next week."

"Is that Tom Kinsella?" Jim Anderson asked.

Dad looked at Jim Anderson. "Do you know him?"

"Not personally, but he used to be quite a football player at the university. Isn't he a . . . a surgeon now?"

"No, he's a blood specialist," Dad said quietly.

"That's right, sure." Jim Anderson looked at me. He still didn't get it.

"It's very nice to see you again, Mr. Anderson," Mom said coldly, giving him the hint to leave. "We appreciate your interest in Paul, but—"

"Not Paul, ma'am, the team. We need him."

I liked Jim Anderson. He was simple and straightforward.

"I'm sure he'd love to play, but we have to get settled first. In addition to many other things, both boys start a new school tomorrow and—"

"School," Larry said disgustedly. "They've only got two weeks of school left, and we have to go to it."

"Yes, you do. You both do," Mom said. "You'll make new friends and in the autumn when you return, you won't be coming back to something new and strange."

"I've got friends already, Mom. On the Wilson Dairy team."

"Please, Paul!"

"Can I ask you when my appointment with Dr. Kinsella is?"

"A week from Wednesday."

I turned to Jim Anderson. "When do you play your games?"

"Mondays and Wednesdays."

"So I miss this Wednesday's game, and Monday's . . . and probably next Wednesday's game too. That's three big games. Why can't you call Dr. Kinsella tonight and move the appointment up to tomorrow?"

"You can't do that to a doctor, Paul," Dad said. "This isn't an emergency."

"It is for the team," the Punk said.

"Larry, go upstairs," Mom said.

"I'll be quiet."

Dad shook his head. "No, I don't believe in anybody being quiet, but this isn't the time or the manner in which to discuss this. Thank you for dropping by, Jim."

Jim Anderson looked uncomfortable. He didn't know what he had stepped into, but he knew it was deep and he knew he hadn't made friends with my parents.

"Well, Paul—if Dr. Kinsella says OK, just give the entry blank to any of the boys on the team. You'll see most of them in school. They almost all go to Sampson Park

School. I guess I'll be moving along. Sorry to have busted in on you like this but the boys were so high on Paul's fast ball and curve, and—well—I—" He looked sideways at Mom, and whatever else he was going to say, he didn't. He sort of waved his hand and went out the door.

"Thanks, Mom," I said. "You were real friendly."

"Why should I have been?"

"Because he's a nice guy and he didn't know I was sick."

"We told him that, Paul, and still he stayed. And you wanted him to. You know, Paul, you're not making this any easier for yourself or for us."

"That's not the point, Mom. The point is—I feel good. I can play baseball again. Baseball didn't make me sick in Texas or California and it won't make me sick here."

"Ssh, both of you," Dad said. "Paul, stop pushing the baseball. Your mother has every right to be worried. As for your coach, I quite agree with you that he's a nice person. If Dr. Kinsella gives his permission then I'll sign your card. But you are going to have to wait until you see him. And that's that."

"So I miss three games in a season that's already a couple of weeks old."

"Is that so awful?"

"Those guys need me. They're not going to make the playoffs unless they get another pitcher."

Dad shook his head, smiling just a little. "You arrived in Arborville a couple of hours ago and already there's an Arborville team that cannot live without you. Well, son, you can live without them. In fact, you may have to live without them. I'm sorry to have to talk this way to you because I think you know better. It was foolish of you to have thrown a ball today; it was foolish of Larry to trick us into going to the park before supper. Now, I would like to put a stop to all further discussion. Your mother and I have a lot of work to do still, and you boys are both going to school in the morning so please go upstairs now and get ready for bed."

"Bed?" Larry was shocked. "It's not even nine o'clock."

"I didn't say go to bed. I said get ready for bed."

There was nothing more to say. Dad didn't put his foot down often, but when he did it came down firmly.

I picked up the orange bag.

"Paul, put that down," Mom said.

"You want it upstairs, don't you? Well, if Larry can carry it in, I can carry it up."

Then before she could say another word, I took the overnight bag upstairs and tossed it on their bed. Then I went into the bedroom, slammed the door shut, jumped up onto the top bunk, and lay there.

It took me a moment to realize I still had something half crumpled in my left hand. I looked at it. It was the entry blank for the baseball league. I smoothed it out and studied it. ARBORVILLE RECREATION BASEBALL LEAGUES, it said on the top. Then DATE. Then: "I_____give permission for my son_____to compete in the____-year-old league. I understand he agrees to abide by the rules of the league. Neither the league nor any of its officials, coaches, or players are to be held responsible in the case of any injury to my son." Then there was a blank and under it was: PARENT/GUARDIAN_____.

It was simple and clear, a passport to life. But I'd have to wait more than a week to find out if I would play. And then suppose Dr. Kinsella said no. Then what?

"Paul?"

"What?"

"Can I come in?"

"It's your room too, dummy."

He opened the door. "I thought you might be asleep."

"Funny."

He came in. "Can I see the entry card?"

"What for?"

"I've got to get one too. Let's see it."

I handed it down to him. He read it. "It's just like the one in California." He handed it back to me. "What are you going to do with it?"

"Nothing . . . yet."

"What do you mean?"

"Forget it."

"Paul, you're going to do something, aren't you?"

"Shut up, Pest."

"You better not."

"I better not what?"

"What you're thinking."

"I'm not thinking anything. I'm supposed to rest. I'm sick."

"Aw, Paul."

"All of a sudden I can't even carry a little suitcase up the stairs."

"Mom can't help that. She worries about you." He got into the lower bunk and lay down.

"Hey, you know something?"

"What?"

"You make a big lump in the mattress."

He poked a finger up into me.

"Cut it out."

"Hey, let's have signals. One poke means let's talk. Two pokes means let's go to sleep. Three could mean let's whistle. Four could mean let's tell jokes. Five—"

"Larry," I growled, "pitchers never take signals from shortstops."

The Punk giggled. "Boy, and were you ever throwing them in the lane, Paul. I had to laugh when Monk got knocked down. Their eyes were really popping out of their heads." He hesitated. "Paul."

"What?"

"Suppose the doctor won't let you play."

I didn't answer. There was no answer.

"It isn't fair," the Punk said. "It just isn't." And then he had the sense to change the subject. "I wonder what the new school's gonna be like. It looks old-fashioned. It's crazy to go with only two weeks left but maybe I'll meet some guys. You know, I don't think this town's gonna be half bad, Paul. Dad's promised me a backboard after he gets permission. . . ."

I was tempted to interrupt and ask my kid brother what would happen if Dad didn't get permission, but I didn't.

". . . Maybe we can get the backboard up tomorrow, Paul. Anyway, if I don't get on a baseball team I'll work on my jump shot. . . ."

And on he rambled about his jump shot and why he'd just as soon shoot baskets as play baseball though he was sure some ten-year-old team needed a hot shortstop and if they didn't there was always the Saturday morning basketball league and pickup baseball games at the park but still he just couldn't believe that a guy who could field and throw as well as he could wouldn't be needed by some team, so everything would be all right.

The Punk had it all figured out. Everything had to fall into place for him. All he had to do was wait for some lucky team to find him.

For me, waiting was disastrous. Waiting was running out of time. I was running out of time.

I listened to my kid brother and stared at the blank entry card in my hand.

7 FALSE ENTRY

LOOKING BACK on it now, I realize that what I did was wrong. But at the time I thought it was right for two reasons: I felt well enough to play ball, and Dad just wasn't going to try to get an earlier appointment with Dr. Kinsella.

At breakfast the next morning, we were all up early to get off to school: Mom, me, and Larry to Sampson Park School, and Dad to the university—with some errands on the way.

"Don't forget you're gonna get permission to put up a backboard today," the Punk reminded him.

"I won't forget."

"Frank, we'll need to go marketing today."

"I know that, Helen."

"Dad, could you call Dr. Kinsella up today and try to get an earlier appointment?"

"Paul, specialists like Dr. Kinsella set up their appointments weeks ahead of time."

"All I'm asking you to do is try."

"I'll try."

"Boys, let's go," Mom said.

To my surprise the Punk protested. "Mom, Paul and I can register at school by ourselves. They know we're coming. You wrote and telephoned, we can do it ourselves."

The Punk knew it wouldn't look good for him if he showed up the first day with his mother in tow. I didn't care one way or another.

"There's probably something for me to sign, Larry."

"We'll bring it home."

"Don't you want me there either, Paul?"

"I don't care. We can do it ourselves but if you want to come—"

The upshot was that Mom stayed home and the Punk and I set off for school, following the same route to the park that we'd followed the other day.

Sampson Park School was an old-fashioned two-story building. In California and Texas we'd gone to modern, one-level schools. This would be different. Another thing that was different was the big soccer game going on in front of the school. I'd never seen anything like that before. There must have been a hundred kids in it: big kids and little kids, athletes and nonathletes, running up and down, kicking up dirt, shrieking. And there was a soccer game within a soccer game because a second ball appeared, and while one wave of kids went one way, a smaller wave went the other way.

"Hey, this is cool," the Pest said, breaking into a trot.

"Where're you going?"

"I'm gonna get into it."

"Don't be an ass. You've never played soccer before."

"Heck, Paul, all you do is kick a ball."

And then, with the supreme confidence of a ten-year-old kid who thinks he's God's gift to sports, the Punk dashed into the middle of the game and started chasing the ball. No one paid any attention to him.

I watched for a few minutes, now and then spotting a kid from the Wilson Dairy team. I don't know how they knew who was on what team. Kids joined the game and left the game. There were no teams. I swear I even saw one kid change sides in the middle of the game—probably to get on the winning side, if there was a winning side.

Suddenly the Punk had the ball and he was dribbling it off his right toe like he had played soccer all his life. He was nimble all right. They started to close in on him so he gave it a good kick, and ran after it, yelling. He was already part of the Arborville scene. Too much a part of it. I waited till the flow came back toward me again and then I stepped onto the field and grabbed him as he came flying by.

"Hey, leggo . . . oh, it's you."

"Yeah, it's me. C'mon, we got to go in and see the principal."

"Oh . . . boy, I forgot. Paul, this is fun."

A bell rang then and that broke up the soccer game. Everyone started running for the building.

"Run, Paul," the Punk shrieked, "we're gonna be late."

I didn't run. How could we be late if we weren't even registered? But the Punk never thought ahead.

We found the principal's office on the second floor. A bunch of kids were in there already, talking and arguing with two clerks. When they were through, one of the clerks asked us what we wanted and I explained who we were and that my mom had called and written from California.

"Oh, yes," she said, "you're the Mather boys. Your parents will have to fill out these forms. Which one of you is Larry?"

"Me."

"You're in Miss Lake's fourth-grade class. Tom, will you show this boy where Miss Lake's class is?"

"Good luck, Punk," I whispered to him. He winked at me. He'd made up his mind that this new town was a setup for him. It was a good attitude to have.

The clerk told me I was in Mrs. Kircher's sixth-grade class, and she got a runner to take me there.

The runner—a kid my age—wanted to know if I knew there were only two weeks of school left, and I told him I knew. He wanted to know why I was here then, and I told him I had nothing else to do. He wanted to know why I didn't go fishing and I told him I didn't like fishing. He wanted to know what I liked and I told him playing baseball. He wanted to know who I was going to play for and I didn't tell him anything.

Besides, at that point we were at Mrs. Kircher's class which you could hear all the way down the hall. The door was open and almost the first kid I saw inside that class was Monk Lawler. Tip Barnett was in the class, too, and two other guys from the team.

When they saw me, those guys started hollering. Just like that. Right in the middle of class.

"Hey, Paul, come on in."

"Is Paul gonna be in our class, Mrs. Kircher?"

"Sit here, Mather."

"That's the kid we were telling you about, Kauffman. He throws harder than Sandy Koufax any day."

"Bull—"

"Quiet, please," the teacher yelled . . . but the noise went on. I was flabbergasted. We sometimes had noisy classes in California, but nothing like this.

Finally, Mrs. Kircher said: "Quiet and take your seats or there'll be no recess."

Those magic words work everywhere. Suddenly there was silence and everyone sat down. Mrs. Kircher smiled at me.

"You must be Paul Mather."

"Yes, ma'am."

"We're glad to have you here, even if there are only two weeks left to the term. I hope the class you were in wasn't as noisy as this one."

"He's from California," Tip Barnett said. "Everyone's noisy there."

The class erupted again. Mrs. Kircher held up her hand. "Do you or do you not want recess?"

Silence.

She turned to me. "Paul, why don't you tell us all something about yourself, where you came from, whether you have brothers and sisters . . ."

"Yeah," Monk Lawler croaked, "speech. Speech."

Everyone started clapping. What a welcome. What a town. I grinned. The funny part was, I'd done the same thing in California. The teacher there had me make a speech.

"Throw your curve," Tip Barnett shouted.

I laughed. It really felt good to know I had friends out there already.

"Quiet," Monk croaked. "The hottest pitcher around is gonna talk. Go ahead, Paul."

I cleared my throat. "My name's Paul Mather. I was born in Texas. When I was in fourth grade we moved to California. My dad's a professor of geology. I've got a little brother who's crazy about basketball. My mom's a housewife. That's it."

Silence, and then Monk said: "That's not enough. We want more."

I could have killed him.

"Tell them about your no-hitters, Paul."

"Tell about your perfect game."

"He's gonna pitch for us, Mrs. Kircher."

"How come?" another boy asked. "You can't sign up a new guy just like that."

"Who says we can't?"

"I say."

Tip and another kid were up on their feet ready to fight. Everyone was yelling. I'd really done a great job introducing myself. I wished I could hide under Mrs. Kircher's desk, unless she was hiding there herself. She wasn't, though; she was pounding it, trying to make order. But this time even the threat of no recess didn't work. So she pulled the ace out of her sleeve and yelled: "Recess. Time for recess."

Everyone piled out happily.

Recesses are the same everywhere. Kids manufacture balls out of pockets and start throwing them around.

Someone always has a bat. I wondered if my folks had thought of the possibility of my being exposed to baseball during school like this. Obviously they hadn't.

This particular recess would not have been a problem, though. A bunch of guys surrounded me the second I got outside and started throwing questions at me.

"Are you really gonna play with the Dairy team? How come?"

"We need a pitcher."

"We got a better team than them."

"Hey, lay off of him. We saw him first."

"Has he signed with the league?"

"Did you turn in the entry card yet, Mather?"

I shook my head.

"Then he's not on your team, Lawler, so what're you talking about?"

"He's gonna be on our team," Monk said grimly, "anyone want to fight about it?"

No one cared to fight Monk.

"Ain't that right, Paul? You're gonna play with us."

"If I play at all," I said quietly.

They all looked at me.

"What d'you mean?"

I took a deep breath. "You see, I got to get a doctor's permission first before my dad will sign his permission."

"What's wrong with you?"

"You look OK to me."

"You should've seen him throw to Monk yesterday."

"Gee, what've you got?"

"It's a fancy disease."

"Hey, how about that?"

"I had pneumonia once. That was pretty fancy."

"Barnett, remember when you had your appendix out? That was fancy."

"Yeah," Tip said, "it hurt."

"Does yours hurt?"

"No."

"Good," Monk said, "so there's no problem then. You see the doctor and he says you go ahead and throw those curve balls for the Dairy team. We got a game tomorrow against Ace Appliance. That's a team we got to beat to make the playoffs."

"Can you see your doctor today?" Tip Barnett asked me.

"My dad's finding out right now."

"Good," Monk said, "because we need you tomorrow."

Larry was home ahead of me for lunch. "Hey, I got a real cool class. How's yours?"

"OK."

"And I'm on a baseball team, Mom. The shortstop they got stinks. They're gonna get me an entry card this afternoon. We play Tuesdays and Fridays."

"Mom, did Dad call Dr. Kinsella yet?"

"I don't know, Paul. Your father's been at the university all morning."

"What about the trust company? He said he was going there and get permission and then buy a backboard today."

"I'm sure he'll be doing that, Larry."

"Could you call him and remind him about Dr. Kinsella, Mom?"

"Paul, I don't want to hear another word about baseball, please. Now, both of you, eat and get back to school."

Even though I wasn't much hungry, I ate and went back to school. That afternoon the kids forgot about me because they had to wrestle with something called negative numbers. I didn't understand what their math was all about, but Mrs. Kircher told me not to worry; she'd talk with me and my parents and find out what I knew and didn't know. It was all the same subject matter, she said, just a different way of approaching it. I didn't know what she was talking about. I didn't care, either.

I rushed home right after school hoping to catch Dad, but he wasn't home yet.

"How can I find out if he called Dr. Kinsella?" I asked Mom.

"You can't until he comes home."

"What about the trust company?" the Punk asked. "Did he get permission from them?"

"Larry, you're becoming a pest. I've really got a lot of work to do now."

Dad came home around five o'clock. He'd bought a big backboard at the lumberyard.

The Punk jumped in the air. "I'll help you put it up. I know how to do it. It's easy."

"I'll help too," I said.

Dad smiled at us. "It's too late to get started on it today, boys. This is going to be a big project. I'll get on it tomorrow. I found a graduate student at the university who'll help me."

"I helped you put it up in California, Dad."

"Paul, it's only a two-man project and this student wants to help me."

"Did you call Dr. Kinsella?"

Dad shook his head. "I didn't get a chance."

"But you had the time to get permission to put up a backboard and then to buy a backboard."

"I was going by the lumberyard on my way home."

Dad could talk his way out of anything. There was no sense pursuing that.

"All right. Could you call him now?"

Dad looked at his watch. "He wouldn't be in his office now."

"Could you at least try?"

"All right."

Dad called the University Hospital. Sure enough, Dr. Kinsella wasn't there.

"Could you try him at home?"

"I couldn't do that."

"Why not?"

"Because you can't bother a doctor at his home about baseball, Paul."

"This isn't baseball, Dad. It's me. That team needs me tomorrow."

"I need you too, Paul."

"Dad, I'm all right."

"We don't know that."

"You won't even try to find out. Call Dr. Kinsella."

"I just did. He's not there."

"Call him at home."

"Paul, you can't bother a doctor at his home about baseball. . . ."

And there we were, back where we started. Then Mom

started up about having to go to the market and the Punk about getting the backboard up as soon as possible and that was the end of Dr. Kinsella.

I knew now I had absolutely nothing to lose by taking action myself.

After supper, Mom and Dad went off to the market. The Punk took off for the park with his glove, hoping to get into a pickup ball game.

"You want to come, Paul?"

"No."

"Don't be angry. Dad'll call that guy tomorrow."

"No, he won't, and we both know it."

Larry nodded. "Well . . . anyway . . . I'll see you later."

"Yeah, have fun."

He took off. I waited till he was out of sight. Then I went into my folks' bedroom and searched around for a fountain pen. I found one. Then I went into our room and got out Jim Anderson's crumpled entry card. First I smoothed it out, and then I carefully filled in the blanks from top to bottom.

On the line where it asked for the signature of Parent/ Guardian, I signed my father's name, doing it quickly to make it look as grown-up and unreadable as possible.

8 SPOTTED!

THAT NIGHT they didn't notice I had stopped bugging them about calling Dr. Kinsella. Either that or they decided to let sleeping dogs lie. Anyway, I didn't say a word about it, and neither did they, which only convinced me more that I'd done the right thing.

The next morning, entry card and four quarters from my piggy bank in my pocket, I went to school. Monk and I caught sight of each other before the bell rang. I turned to Larry. "I'll see you later, Pest."

He took the hint and skipped off. He was getting only too glad to be rid of me.

"Did you see the doctor?" Monk asked me.

"Yeah."

"Well?"

"It's OK. I can play. I got the entry card here."

"Let's see."

I gave him the card. Monk studied it and then grinned. "Great. This is it. This is gonna help us go all the way. I'll take it over to Jim at the firehouse right after school. He's a fireman over on Stadium Boulevard. He's got some extra uniforms there. I'll bring one over to your house right away—"

"Monk, I've got a better idea. Why don't you bring the uniform back to your house and I'll change there? It'll save time later."

Since I was making things easier for him, Monk didn't ask any questions.

But fooling Monk, who wanted me to play, was easy. Fooling my folks, who didn't want me to play, would be harder.

What I had to do was figure out the best way to get myself out of the house for over two hours, and at supper time, too. So while everyone else in Mrs. Kircher's class was puzzling over math problems, I was puzzling over my own special problem. Neither the class nor I seemed to be doing very well.

At lunch time, Mom was cheerful, probably because I wasn't making any more noises about Dr. Kinsella. The Punk was cheerful, too, because Dad had called to say he would be coming home with a graduate student who would help him put up the backboard that afternoon.

I thought hard about that. I wondered if my way out of the house might not be through a backboard.

How to solve my problem occupied me most of the afternoon in school. Mrs. Kircher left me alone while the class worked on Indian names in Michigan. By the time school was over, I thought I knew how to get out of the house.

Dad was working in the driveway with his graduate student. They had sawed up some two-by-fours and were working on getting the heavy backboard up the ladder. Then they'd have to hold it in place while someone bolted it to the supports.

"Can I help?" I asked.

"No, Paul," Dad said, "it's a two-man job."

I watched them struggle for a few minutes and then I went inside. Mom was lining shelves in the kitchen. I took a deep breath.

"Hey, I'm starving," I said. "Can I make myself a sandwich?"

"Of course you can," Mom said, surprised but pleased. Ordinarily, I had no appetite at all.

I made myself a salami sandwich and had a glass of milk. I wasn't the least bit hungry but I wolfed it down. "Can I make another one?"

"You'll have no appetite for supper, Paul."

"But I'm starving *now*, Mom."

She smiled. "Go ahead. I haven't seen you eat like this in a long time."

Aware that she was watching me, I did it up proper. I had another salami sandwich, a wedge of cheese, some cookies, and an apple. And more milk. Mom was practically bug-eyed, but happy. I looked at the clock. Almost four. Time to get moving. I gobbled up the apple.

"Paul, you amaze me," Mom said.

"I'm gonna go help Dad put up the backboard now."

"Please don't."

"Mom, there's nothing else for me to do."

"Why don't you take a walk and explore the neighborhood?"

Beautiful. She wanted me away from the house so I wouldn't be tempted to help Dad with the heavy work.

I shrugged. "Explore? Well, OK, what time do I have to be back?"

"We'll eat around six fifteen."

"Suppose I see something interesting. Can I keep walking? I mean, I just ate a lot and I probably won't be hungry again at six fifteen."

This was it. The crucial moment. She had to agree to this or all would be lost.

She agreed. She smiled. "All right, Paul, but do get back before it gets dark."

It wouldn't work for every game, but it was working now, and as the coaches always say, you got to play them one game at a time.

"Thanks, Mom."

I hugged her. She held me and kissed me. I felt a little guilty. I started up the stairs.

"Where are you going?"

"To the bathroom."

I went into our room and got out my baseball glove and my baseball shoes. I wrapped them in my windbreaker. As I went out the front door I could hear Mom whistling cheerfully. Now I really felt guilty.

In the driveway, Dad's graduate student was on the garage roof holding onto the backboard. Dad was on the ladder trying to prop it up, and a man I'd never seen before, I guess he was a neighbor, was telling Dad he'd bring his stepladder over and support the other end of the backboard.

"Good," I heard Dad say, "then I can get on the roof with Bill."

So much for a two-man operation, I thought bitterly, and immediately stopped feeling guilty.

Monk Lawler lived on the corner of Cambridge and Lincoln in a big old frame house. He must have been watching for me out the window, because by the time I hit the top step of his porch, he had opened the door and was standing there, uniform in hand. He was in his uniform already.

"It's about time you got here. I was getting a little worried."

"It was hard getting away."

"Man, when there's a ball game, you just take off. I sure hope you're not that slow on the diamond."

I laughed. "Let's see the uniform."

He tossed it at me. "You better hustle into it. C'mon, you can change in our downstairs bathroom and leave your clothes there."

"Who is it, Monk?" a woman's voice called out.

"It's the new kid on our team, Ma. Paul Mather. He's going to change here."

"All right, but you both better hurry. Your father said to be at the parking lot at a quarter to five."

"We'll be there, Ma. C'mon, Paul, hustle. You got pants, cap, shirt, socks. Those pants are gonna be too small. You got long legs all right. Do you run track?"

"No."

Monk sat down on the edge of the bathtub while I changed into the uniform.

"Basketball?"

"No."

"Football?"

"No. Just baseball."

"Can you hit?"

"I got a hit once a couple of years ago."

I said it deadpan. Monk looked at me to see if I was joking, and he must have decided I was because he started to laugh.

He laughed long enough for me to realize he was laughing at the way my uniform fitted me, which was no fit at all. Short pants, wide shirt. Well, a wide shirt never hindered a pitcher, but it wasn't right to look silly around the legs.

"Next game I want a new uniform."

Monk laughed. "You give orders like a pitcher. I hope you're as good as you talk. C'mon, get your cap on, we've got to run."

"Walk."

"We're late, man."

"They'll wait."

"Mather, you beat all."

"I haven't lost yet."

Monk stared at me. "You're kidding."

"Nope."

"Geez," he said, "we'll walk."

Once outside, however, he instinctively started running. Monk was a hustler. Kids who hustle on the diamond hustle off the diamond, too.

"C'mon!"

"I'm saving it for the game."

"Pitchers need good legs, don't they?"

"I'm not going to run the ball over the plate. Worry about my arm instead."

He stopped and looked concerned. "Does it hurt?"

"No. It feels great."

He made a face. "Then let's go." He started trotting again. He couldn't help it. I let him go. When he saw I wasn't following him, he waited.

"You're pretty sure of yourself, Mather."

I wasn't, but I wasn't going to tell him that. When you've spent months in a hospital bed, you learn to play things close to the vest. Pitchers have to do that anyway, even if they aren't sick. They can't let a batter know what's coming; they can't let the other team know they're losing their stuff or getting tired. You got to keep up a front.

So Monk walked with me and pretty soon we were at the park. Monk spotted the Dairy team in the parking lot.

"That red truck is Jim's pickup. We get to go in that. We bang the sides and yell at people. It's a gas. There's my dad. He's looking our way. I'm going." He started to run again, but slowed to a walk as he remembered.

He hesitated. I could see he was debating with himself. Then he came out with it. "When you were sick, Paul. How sick were you?"

Now it was my turn to hesitate. It wouldn't be fair to Monk, to any of them, to tell them the truth. It was my problem, not theirs.

"Oh . . . pretty sick."

"Like," he paused, "did you almost die?"

I shook my head.

"It's OK for you to play ball then, isn't it? I mean, the doctor said it was OK."

"Sure."

Monk was silent. "I've never been really sick."

"It's no fun."

"I guess not."

"Hey, you two," Jim Anderson's voice boomed across the park, "put on the gas."

"Let's go," Monk said, and this time we both ran. Having a coach tell you to run is a lot different than a buddy. I was puffing by the time we reached the parking lot. I could pace myself on the mound, but not in a parking lot.

Jim Anderson took my four quarters and said he was glad to have me on the team. He was sorry the uniform didn't fit, but he'd see what he could do about getting some bigger pants. He introduced me to Monk's father, a tall hard-faced man who Monk was going to look like when he got older. Then I met all the guys on the team. Jim Anderson insisted on formal introductions even though it used up time. "You should know who's behind you when you start pitching," he said.

Monk made the introductions.

"This weird-looking kid is our right fielder Stu Abels. The fat kid next to him is Kenny Banks, our third baseman. Ugly here is Cliff Borton who pretends he plays first base. Bob Gordon makes the errors in left field and Warren Miller bounces them off his head in center. You know Tip. He's your catcher and you'll never get a worse one. Jim Hakken plays shortstop and pitches. Trouble is he can't do either. These other guys are on the team, too, but we try to keep them out till the last inning." Monk introduced me to the subs. As far as I was concerned, everyone looked alike: chewing gum, freckles . . . they looked like the kids in Texas and California.

They all started asking me questions at once, like where had I come from, what kinds of pitches did I throw, did I know my pants were too short and my shirt too wide?

Jim stopped it. "Hey, you can ask him questions after the game. Now we got to go over to Clinton School Diamond. Paul, you know I've never even seen you throw a ball and I've got you down as starting pitcher, so when we get there I want to warm you up. Are your folks coming?"

"No."

"Well, you thank your dad for me for getting the permission so fast from the doctor. Now, let's see, who's coming in the pickup and who's going with Mr. Lawler?"

"Pickup, pickup, pickup," everyone sang out as their hands shot up.

"OK," Mr. Lawler said, "I'll follow behind and pick up everyone who falls out of the pickup."

The guys started climbing into the truck. I put one hand on top and a foot on a tire. A helping hand came down from the truck. It was Monk's.

"Easy up," he said, and helped me up into the truck.

"I'm out of shape," I said apologetically.

"That's OK," Stu Abels said, "we got lots of guys who can climb into trucks, but we got no one who can pitch."

"Cut it out, Abels," Jim Hakken said.

"Except Hakken, I mean."

"Is the equipment bag up there?" Jim Anderson called out.

"Yep."

"OK, look out for it. And no banging on the sides. You do that only if we win."

"That means we don't get to do it."

"Who said that?"

"We can beat Ace."

"With Red Kelly pitching? Are you kidding?"

"Mather will make Kelly look like a Girl Scout," Tip Barnett said.

"You ever seen a Girl Scout pitch, Tippy?"

"Pitch cookies."

"Hey, Paul, are you really as fast as Monk and Tip say?"

"He's faster," Monk said.

"Hang on, everyone," Jim Anderson yelled out the window.

The truck started and then lurched forward, spilling us against each other.

"Hey, get off me."

"You're on me, clown."

"He ought to get this thing fixed."

"Naw, I like starting like that."

"Let's go, Dairies!"

"Hey, Jim said not to bang the sides."

"I didn't. My hand slipped."

The guys on the truck laughed, and then there was more laughter as we bounced against each other. The truck turned right onto Baldwin, and came up to the corner of Baldwin and Granger. I wasn't laughing. My heart was in my mouth. Did the way to Clinton School Diamond lead past our house where my dad was outside in the driveway putting up the backboard? I hadn't thought of this.

The truck turned left and went up to the corner of

Granger and Ferdon. Our house was just down the lane there. If we went straight ahead, I'd have to duck way down.

We were stopped at a stop sign. A car went by. Then someone said, "Hey, Mather, isn't that your kid brother?"

I turned around. There, standing on the northeast corner of Ferdon and Granger, bouncing a basketball, was the Punk. He was grinning up at the guys in the truck who were calling down insults on him and all basketball players. He kept grinning and dribbling in place and then our eyes met. It was too late to duck. For the first time in his life, Larry missed the ball. It fell at his feet and rolled down the sidewalk.

"Double dribble!"

"Hey, kid, who taught you to dribble?"

Larry stared at me: at my cap, my baseball shirt, at the words WILSON DAIRY printed across it.

I felt sick in my stomach.

Then the truck made a right-hand turn, away from the lane.

As we turned, I shook my head at him. I tried to say silently, "Don't tell them, please. . . ." I don't know whether he understood. He just kept staring at me until we had completed the turn and my back was toward him. Then he was gone . . . and I was gone.

Someone tapped my shoulder. It was Monk. "That *was* your kid brother, wasn't it?"

"Yes."

"He looked surprised to see you."

I didn't say anything. There wasn't anything to say. The only thing to do now was pray silently that the Punk would have the sense not to tell Mom and Dad. It wouldn't do them any good; it wouldn't do me any good.

The truck picked up speed. The guys all banged the sides with their hands and yelled at pedestrians. The only two guys not horsing around were me and Monk Lawler. I just stood there holding on, and Monk just stood there looking at me, and I knew he knew what I'd done to get in uniform and play today.

9 TIME OUT #2

"ALL RIGHT, LAD," Nurse Brophy said, "put that tape recorder away. It's medication time."

"Brophy, you were just by with it. I took it already."

"Did you now?" she said, swinging the medicine tray over my bed. "You wouldn't be trying to take advantage of an old nurse, would you, lad? Put that thing away now."

"I'm not done talking into it."

"You've talked too much already, if you ask me. I never heard of such nonsense. Tape recorders in a hospital. You'd think you had something important to say."

If I could get Brophy talking, she might forget about the medication.

"It is important, Brophy. I'm telling my story."

"*Your* story? You're twelve years old. You're not old

enough to have a story. Wait till you're my age and then you might have a story."

"How old are you, Brophy?"

Keep talking, Brophy.

"Old enough to know when someone's trying to distract me. Lean forward."

She had the rubber cap. I leaned toward her and she pulled it over my head. It was supposed to prevent your hair from falling out. The medicine did that to you, in addition to making you feel awful.

"Would you like to hear one of my tapes, Brophy? I'm almost up to the game I pitched for the Wilson Dairy team."

"I'm not interested in baseball, lad. It's an idiotic game. People stand around wearing gloves while someone with a stick tries to hit a ball. It doesn't take much brains to play that sport. Now football, that's something else. There's a game for you. Now sit up, here's—"

"Brophy, hitting a baseball coming at you a hundred miles an hour is—"

"—Your water, and—"

"—The hardest thing in the world. Baseball's a lot more interesting than football. It's—"

"—Your pills."

"Brophy, there's only supposed to be three."

"Four, and get them over with."

"Brophy, these pills are bigger than usual."

"They're exactly the same size. Don't dawdle, lad. Waiting only makes it worse. One, two, three, now."

There was nothing for it but to take them. Increased dosage was increased discomfort and increased nausea and increased burning and itching. I'd been on the increased

83

dosage for a week now and it was only making me sicker. I was tired all day long, and after the medicine I was nauseous and sick.

It was pill, water, swallow; pill, water, swallow; pill, water, swallow; pill, water, swallow. I was good at it now. A regular pill-taking machine. Practice makes perfect.

Now I had about twenty minutes before the effects started hitting me.

Brophy took the paper cup from me. Her voice softened. "That's my lad. It wasn't so bad, was it?"

"It will be."

"Where are you in your story, Paul?"

Now our roles were reversed. She was trying to distract *me*, get my mind off the discomfort that was on its way. Well, I'd go along with it. About the only thing that could get my mind off the aftereffects of the medicine was baseball. Whenever the nausea hit, I tried hard to remember part of a baseball game somewhere, in Texas, California, or even here.

"Where was I? I was up to the game I pitched against Ace Appliance."

"Aha. The big game."

"The only game, you mean."

"There'll be more, lad."

"Do you think so, Brophy?"

"I most certainly do."

"You know, Brophy, we play them again this season. We play each team twice. Brophy, get me the schedule again. It's on the table. It's that orange sheet."

"This one?"

"Yes. Read it to me. When do we play Ace Appliance again?"

"Who're you?"

"Oh, Brophy, we're Wilson Dairy; you know that."

She smiled. She knew it all right. I told her twice a day I pitched for the Wilson Dairy team.

"Let's see, Wilson Dairy versus Ace Appliance. You play June twenty-fourth."

"Brophy," I said disgustedly, "that was the first game. That was a month ago."

Brophy laughed. "Of course. That was the day you blessed us with your presence in the hospital. Let's see, Wilson Dairy–Ace Appliance. Here it is. You play them again on August first, at Sampson Park, diamond number two."

"What's today, Brophy?"

"The twentieth."

"How many days in July, Brophy?"

"The questions you ask, lad. Let's see. Thirty days hath September, April, June, and November . . . thirty-one days in July."

"That gives me twelve days to get back, Brophy. I can do it, don't you think?"

"Paul, you're getting excited. Lie back."

"No, I can be back in uniform then. In California when I got well, Brophy, it was overnight. That's how these remissions work. One day you're sick and the next day you're well and you can do anything. I'm going to be back for that second game against Ace Appliance. It's a revenge game for me, Brophy. I've got to get back."

"Shsh, before I get you a different kind of pill."

"What are you doing?"

"Lowering the shades. You'll be doing yourself a big favor, lad, if you're asleep when the pills hit."

"I can't sleep now, Brophy. I've got something to look forward to. The revenge game against Ace."

"There'll be no revenge game for you unless you sleep. I've got to go now. Is there anything else you want?"

"Is Tom around?"

"Dr. Kinsella is in the hospital somewhere, I believe."

"Would you ask him about August first? Please, Brophy?"

"Paul, will you try to sleep?"

"Please, Brophy, please."

"If I see him I'll ask him. Now you get some sleep. I'll be right down the hall. You can ring if you need me."

She left then, a tough old gray-headed nurse. I listened to her footsteps going down the hall. She had heavy steps; Tom's were light. I'd only been here about a month but it felt like I'd been here years. August first. Twelve days from now. Twelve days in which to get better and get back for that game. I had to get back. The first game against Ace had been a disaster for me, and for the team. The worst part was, I could remember every detail of it, from going there in the truck to the awful mess in the middle of the second inning.

10 BIG GAME

WE WERE in the truck, Larry had spotted me, and Monk knew something was wrong. So while everyone else was banging the sides of the pickup and yelling at pedestrians, Monk was whispering to me: "Your folks don't know you're playing today, do they?"

It never occurred to me to lie to him. Either he was with me or he wasn't. Now was a good time to find out.

"No."

"How come?"

"They won't let me play till I see the doctor."

"How come your dad signed the entry card, then?"

I took a deep breath. The truck rocked along. I held on tight. One truth leads to another.

"He didn't."

"You mean—you signed his name?"

"Yes."

"You're crazy."

"I had to."

"Paul, if the Ace coach ever finds this out, he'll make us forfeit the game."

I hadn't thought of that, but I knew what the answer had to be: "Who's going to tell him?"

I was tossing the ball right back at him. Monk was silent.

"Look," I said, "you yourself told me we didn't have a chance to beat Ace unless you had another pitcher. So what do we have to lose?"

Monk saw it. At least this way we had a fighting chance.

"I know it was the wrong thing to do, Monk, but I'm only saving time for us. I'm supposed to see Dr. Kinsella next week. I'm sure he'll let me play. All I'm doing is working it so I play earlier and get to help you guys when you need it."

It made sense and Monk knew it. He looked at me. "How do you feel now?"

"I feel great, man. As good as you."

Which was the truth. I did feel good. The important thing now was that I'd convinced Monk of the rightness of doing wrong. By the time we got to the diamond at Clinton School, old Monk was pounding the sides of the truck and yelling just like everyone else. So was I.

In Texas and California we played in miniature big league parks. There was a fence in the outfield with advertising on it, and a small grandstand. Here in Arborville, games were played mostly on elementary and junior high school diamonds where fans—parents, kid brothers, sisters—brought their own chairs and blankets and sat along the sidelines. Only the city parks had stands.

A very unimpressive elementary school diamond was the first thing I saw as Jim bounced the truck up onto the grass. I had the feeling the truck would stop as jerkily as it had started and everyone would pile up against everyone else. I held on tight to the side. I wasn't supposed to be bumping into people, or anything for that matter. In California the doctors had told me to avoid cuts and collisions, so had Dr. Kinsella here last February when we'd flown in for the exam. As a matter of fact one of the nice things about being a pitcher was that you could avoid cuts and collisions. In theory, you were alone on the mound.

The truck stopped hard. I leaned in and held on. Monk flew by me and landed on Bob Gordon, the left fielder.

"Sorry," Monk croaked, and gave me a dirty look. He had figured on me as a cushion.

"Hey, Jim, fix the brakes," someone yelled.

"They are fixed," Stu Abels, the right fielder said, "that's the trouble."

"C'mon," Monk growled, "those guys are warming up already. Let's shake it."

He was the first out of the truck. I was right behind him. Monk located a ball and tossed it to me. "Warm up."

"Hey," Tip Barnett said, "I warm up Mather."

A ball bag spilled open on the ground. Hands came out of nowhere to grab the balls.

Across the diamond, the Ace team was loosening up.

"I wonder what time those guys got here."

"Last night," Stu Abels said.

"They look tired," Bob Gordon said.

"Don't you wish it. Red Kelly never looks tired."

"How many innings has he got, Monk?"

"I think four. He pitched three against Michigan Pharmacy."

"How'd he do?"

"Struck out six guys. He one-hit them."

"Ouch."

"Heck, Mather can go seven."

"Can you, Paul?"

"Mather can strike out twenty-one in seven innings."

"Knock it off," Monk growled. "We're not counting on Paul to do it for us. We got to hit Kelly."

"With a brick."

"Funny, Abels."

Jim Anderson came over and watched me throw to Tip. "How's it feel, Paul?"

"Fine, sir."

"No aches or pains?"

"No."

"Keep throwing easy. If it feels all right, I'll start you. I won't pitch you too long."

"I can go seven."

"Sure you can. But this is your first time out and I don't want you to go seven."

I couldn't tell him I wanted all the baseball I could get right away. Who knew what tomorrow would bring? I couldn't tell him that and I didn't want to.

After about a dozen more lob throws to Tip, Jim asked me if I was ready to throw harder. I nodded.

"Let me borrow your glove, Tip," Jim said. "I want to get a feel of this."

Jim changed places with Tip and went down in a squat. I pumped and threw a fast ball.

90

"Nice," Jim said, smiling, and zinged it back at me with a little flip of his wrist. Had he been a major league catcher or something? He had a fantastic wrist throw.

I pumped, rocked, and Jim grinned as I fired my fast ball into his mitt. Mr. Lawler came over and he was smiling, and some of the other fathers, too.

"What'd I tell you, Dad?" Monk croaked happily.

After I'd thrown some fast balls and some curves, Jim stood up. "That's a nifty curve ball you've got there. Who taught you that?"

"A coach."

"Doesn't hurt you, does it?"

"No."

Jim smiled. "Well, it looks like we had a little luck at last. Hey, what're you guys doing standing around and watching? Paul's not watching you. He's warming up. Did you guys come to watch or play?"

Stu Abels laughed. "If he throws like that in the game, we'll be watching, too."

I realized then that the whole Dairy team had stopped warming up and was watching me. I also realized that across the diamond, the Ace Appliance team had been watching my pitching demonstration, too.

The next thing I knew, the Ace Appliance coach was walking over and greeting Jim while I warmed up with Tip.

"See you got a new pitcher, Jim."

"That's right, Doug. How many innings has Red got today?"

"Only four. Nothing for you to worry about. Who's your new boy?"

"Paul Mather. We just signed him up."

"Rules say you can't sign anyone up after the season starts, Jim."

"Check Section 9, Doug. If a boy moves into Arborville from outside the school district, then he's eligible. Paul came in from California."

The Ace coach nodded. I could tell he knew everything Jim had just told him. In a small city word travels fast. But he was being a coach, trying hard to find something wrong with the other team. He changed his approach.

"He looks older than twelve, Jim."

Jim Anderson laughed. "You mean he throws older than twelve."

The Ace coach laughed, too. "I guess maybe that's what I mean. Anyway, you got a birth certificate for him?"

"Come on, Doug. We don't need that. I've got his father's signature on the entry card. His age is on that. That's usually good enough, isn't it?"

"I guess so," the Ace coach said, reluctantly.

Jim Anderson took out the entry permission card on which I had forged my father's name. Monk and I looked at each other.

"Want to see it?" Jim said.

"No. I believe you. It just doesn't seem fair. A real pitcher moves into town and you land him."

"It's about time we had some luck. You want the field first?"

"Might as well." The Ace coach looked at me. "I could see that curve break from across the diamond, son. You'll hurt your arm throwing a ball that way."

"He'll hurt your guys first," Stu Abels said, and our team laughed.

The Ace coach left, and Jim Anderson put the entry

card back in his pocket. I relaxed and went on warming up. It had been close. Only Monk and I knew how close that had been. What neither of us knew, however, was that it wouldn't be long before the entry card came out of Jim's pocket again.

11 FROM HERO TO GOAT

FROM A PITCHER's point of view, the beauty of baseball is its simplicity. You are trying to throw a ball past a kid who is trying to hit it with a bat.

There are other things happening like fielding and base running, bunting and double plays, and so on, but they're just extras. The only thing that matters in baseball is the guy on the mound and the guy in the batter's box.

I was the guy on the mound and this was where I lived. It was what I lived for. Behind me, I could hear my teammates:

"Hey, big Paul."

"Show 'em where you're from, Paul."

"Blow it by him, Paulo."

On the first base side I could hear my opponents:

"Hey, skinny, you can't pitch."

"Spindleshanks, get some meat on you."

"Don't turn sideways, pitch, we'll never see you."

In front of me, I could hear two voices. One belonged to my catcher, Tip Barnett. "No batter, Paul. Pitch to me, Paul. Pitch to my glove, Paul."

The other belonged to the ump.

"Play ball!"

A short freckle-faced kid, his jaw moving up and down with a wad of bubble gum, stepped into the box and took a stance way up front. A bunter, a good runner, a good eye, a battler. The lead-off men of the world all looked alike, I thought.

I glanced over to see where my third baseman was playing. Kenny Banks was even with the bag. Close for the majors, but deep for how the kid in the batter's box was standing and for what I was going to throw him. I waved Kenny in. He didn't want to come in.

"Move in," I said.

I knew the batter wouldn't get around on my fast ball, but Kenny wasn't taking any chances. Third basemen feel naked and lonely playing up close to the batter.

"Move," I ordered.

He moved in a few feet, reluctantly. That would have to do until he came to trust me.

"Have a good look, Dickie," the Ace coach called down from the third base coaching box, reminding Dickie that he was not to swing at the first pitch. He was to see what the new guy had to offer. After all, throwing on the sidelines was one thing, throwing in a game was another. I could be nervous. I was new. First game. A walk was as good as a hit.

I may have been new to Arborville, but I wasn't new to a pitcher's mound or to a batter crouching in a box. I wasn't nervous, I was just very, very grateful to be there.

Dickie blew a bubble and waved his bat at me. Tip went down into a squat. He and I had agreed on four signs: one finger was a fast ball, two fingers a curve, three with a waggle (to make sure I didn't think it was two) was a change-up, or any off-speed pitch, and a fist meant to waste one. Waggled away from the batter it meant waste it outside, toward the batter meant waste it inside.

Tip gave me one finger. I nodded. We'd agreed to start out with fast balls to see how the control went and if I could get a rhythm. Once you got your fast ball past batters, you could do all kinds of things with off-speed pitches and change-ups and curves. But you couldn't work any of them unless your bread and butter fast ball was working for you.

I pumped, rocked, and fired. The kid blinked at it.

"Strike," the ump called, and clicked his indicator, looking at it to make sure it worked.

My guys yelled all at once as though the air came rushing out of them. They probably had been holding their breaths at that.

I grinned at Tip. My arm felt fine. My shoulder felt fine.

Behind me, Monk croaked: "That's humming them, Paul."

Tip Barnett carefully threw the ball back at my chest so I didn't have to reach for it. Some catchers don't care

96

where or how they throw it back and you use up a lot of energy fielding their throws.

Dickie stepped out of the box and looked at his coach who told him to hit away. "All you got to do is meet it," he said. Coaches always made it sound easy.

Dickie stepped back in, still way up front in the box, figuring to jump the ball. That far up, he'd have a hard time coming around.

Tip called for another fast ball. Dickie was swinging when the ball smacked into Tip's mitt.

My guys yelled, and Dickie stepped out of the box to get himself together. He wasn't looking at his coach anymore. He had to think what he was doing wrong, he had to protect the plate, get around on the fast ball. He was a ball player, so he began working it out. His hands moved up the handle of the bat. He'd swing with a choked bat. It would help him get around on it. Next, he'd move back in the box a little. And that he did. I gave Dickie an A for effort, and wondered if Tip had seen the changes and would call for something else other than a fast ball.

Tip either hadn't seen Dickie's new stance or he wanted to stick with a winning pitch. He signaled for another fast ball. I shook it off. Tip gave me the fist outside. No, thank you, Tippy. I'm not wasting pitches today, not knowing how long I can go.

Tip signaled the curve. I nodded.

The Ace team jeered me from their bench. They thought I was putting them on with signals.

Dickie held his choked bat high. He was ready to chop down on the fast ball. I rocked, pumped, gave him the same big fast ball motion, and floated a slow curve right at him. Dickie started to swing, held up, hung in there until he thought the ball was going to hit him on his left shoulder and then he bailed out. The ball curved over the inside corner.

"Strike three," the ump shouted. Tip whipped the ball down to Kenny Banks and around the horn it went with the guys chirping and the outfield singing: "Way to chuck. Way to throw. That's mud in his eye, big Paul."

Dickie was still standing in the batter's box looking at the ump.

"That, son, was a curve ball," the ump said gently.

Dickie nodded. He wasn't disputing the call; he just wanted it explained. He turned and looked at me for a second, and then went back to the bench and threw his bat in the dirt. Our fans clapped, theirs were strangely silent. Jim Anderson, enjoying himself, was marking his score sheet.

Kenny Banks underhanded the ball to me. "How far in should I play, Paul?"

"Another six feet."

Kenny moved in. Kenny was my man now.

I thought their number two batter might try to bunt. He was a lefty and lefties usually tried drag bunting against my fast ball. To my surprise, this kid was up there to hit. He took three good healthy cuts and went back to their bench, shaking his head. That brought up my opposite number—their pitcher Red Kelly. He was a big red-headed boy with alert eyes and big ears. He looked like a farm kid. I wondered if he was a real pitcher or just a kid with a strong arm. He looked like a nice guy. And he looked dangerous at the plate. They were batting him third, so he couldn't be too bad. He took his stance deep in the box and held his hands down at the end of the bat. Long ball hitter.

Tip called for the fast ball and I fed Red one outside. He leaned in and then pulled his bat back to watch it go by. Nothing wrong with him there. I came back with the same pitch but this time we caught the corner. Red had leaned again. He was maybe getting a rhythm with my pitches, leaning into them. But he wasn't quite ripe yet. I decided to gamble with the same pitch again, hoping for the corner. I threw. Red leaned and watched it nip the corner again. One ball, two strikes, and Red was ready now— ripe and ready.

Tip grinned at me. He knew what was going to happen. He signaled for the fast ball again but now he put his target inside. I rocked, pumped, and fired. Red leaned without thinking, and the ball zipped by inside around his knees.

"Strike three!" the ump shouted.

Red opened his mouth to say something, but Tip flipped the ball up at him and we all ran in. Not all of us. I walked. Jim Hakken smacked me on the back, so did Cliff Borton. Easy, guys, I thought.

"How's it feel, Paul?" Monk asked.

"Fine."

"Miller, Lawler, Hakken, Banks," Jim Anderson called out. "Let's get some hits. Way to throw, Paul. How's the arm feel?"

"Great."

"Oh, boy," Stu Abels said. "We're gonna go all the way now. There isn't anyone gonna hit Paul."

"Did you see old Kelly's face when Paul slipped that one inside on him?"

"Old Kelly," Bob Gordon chuckled, "he ain't used to being treated like that."

"And what a curve you threw Molino. He thought it was gonna hit him."

"You got to show me how you throw that, Paul," Jim Hakken said.

"I will."

"Let's go," Jim Anderson called out. "A little hit, Warren. Start things off."

I put on my windbreaker and sat down on the bench to watch Red Kelly. I wanted to study how he pitched, what his weaknesses were. You could learn a lot by watching a guy closely.

Stu Abels sat down next to me. "Way to throw, Paul."

"Thanks, Stu. But that was just half an inning."

"Yeah, but you got them thinking. Look at Red. He keeps sneaking looks over at you."

It was true. Red Kelly kept glancing at me from the pitcher's mound. I wondered at that. Pitchers didn't usually do that. Was Red *too* alert? Was he going to hear every noise, every wisecrack? Was Red going to have rabbit ears and rabbit attention? Could we distract him, get him off his concentration?

Red finished the last of his warm-up throws. Their catcher threw down to second, a high arching throw.

"We can run on him," Stu said, "but Red's pretty smart about keeping you close, so it evens out."

Red kicked some dirt around the mound, made a spot for his left foot to come down, and then he was ready to pitch. He glanced at me again, almost as if he was saying: You were pretty good, now watch me.

I watched. He was a fast worker and a hard thrower and

that was it. He was big and strong and in a few years he'd end up in the outfield. Pitching is more than throwing hard.

But right now, in the twelve-year-old league, it was good enough.

Red blew the ball by Warren Miller. Warren, swinging late, got a piece of the ball only once, sending a skidding grounder foul down the first base line, scaring some fans behind first.

Monk was up number two, and watching him I knew he'd be a tough out. He was cool and calm and swung with a choked bat. Any pitcher would have to battle to get him out. Monk took Red to three and two before he popped up to the third baseman.

That brought up Jim Hakken who was playing shortstop. Jim was a pitcher, a shortstop, an anything. Which meant he was a natural athlete, and from the way he swung a bat, he looked like a natural hitter. He stood deep in the box and broke his wrists gracefully. He even looked good striking out, which he did, and as they came off the field, Red Kelly gave me a grin as if to say: There, I did it too.

I'm on your mind, Red, I thought, and grinned back at him.

I took off my windbreaker.

"One second, Paul," Jim Anderson said to me. "I'm counting on you to let me know when you get tired."

"I will," I said, but I didn't see how I'd ever get tired . . . not from pitching.

The second inning was more of the same. Their first baseman was up in the clean-up spot and he turned out to swing with a choked bat. I knew then they had instructions just to lay wood on the ball. Those are not bad instructions if all the pitcher is doing is firing fast balls at you, but I was throwing change-ups and curves and I could pitch off-speed to spots, so sticking a bat into the strike zone wasn't going to mean a whole lot.

I sent an off-speed fast ball to number four and sure enough he chopped down on it, bouncing a ball right in front of the plate. Tip had to wait for it to come down and when it did he grabbed it and fired to first. An easy out, but the Ace team was shouting.

"That's hitting it, Mike," someone yelled.

Tip laughed. So did Monk. "Yeah, that's hitting it, Mike. Way to whack them, Mike."

"Aw shut up, Lawler," someone from their bench called out.

Monk grinned at them. He liked riling people. He'd be a good man in a fight, I thought. Quick and mean. I was glad he was on my team.

Number five waved a choked bat at me. I blew a fast one by him. Then I was wide with a fast ball, and then I gave him two curves for strikes. They weren't particularly good curves. In fact, the second one hung up there and he could have belted it, but he acted as though he'd never seen a curve ball before, which I guess he hadn't. Not many kids throw curves. It's not supposed to be good for your arm. You're supposed to wait till you're fifteen or sixteen. But I wasn't waiting for anything.

Their next batter was a lefty. I waved Kenny Banks in closer and I waved Bob Gordon in left over toward the line. Outfielders think that when a lefty comes up, you should automatically move toward right field. Not so. It depends on how the kid stands in the box and what you're throwing him. This kid had his right foot toward the plate. He was a slice hitter. Maybe he could pull, but it didn't look like it, and I'd feed him fast balls outside anyway.

He watched my first fast ball cut the corner for a strike. Then I gave him the big motion and threw my change-up. I didn't put it where I wanted it. In fact, it was high, but the kid couldn't stop himself. He was way out in front of it, and fell down. He got up red-faced.

"Hey, Morgan, are you seasick?" Monk called out.

"Morgan, tie your laces."

Morgan dug in. I could see him psyching himself up for every pitch at once. Tip called for the change-up again. It was a brilliant call. Tip was a thinking catcher.

I gave the motion and threw the change-up again, and again Morgan fell down swinging. The side was out.

"Oh, beautiful, baby."

"Way to go, man."

Jim Hakken smacked me on the back. So did Kenny Banks. I tried to avoid them but couldn't. Monk Lawler came over to me as I put on my windbreaker.

"Can you last?"

"Yeah, if the guys stop hitting me on the back."

Monk laughed. He thought I was kidding.

"Banks, Gordon, Barnett, Abels," Jim Anderson called out. "Let's hit this guy. He's nothing but speed."

Kenny Banks had a stance you didn't see often. It was like he'd been sitting in a chair, and you removed the chair from under him and he was still sitting there. A coiled spring, a line drive hitter when his timing was on. An easy out when it was off.

Red wiped his brow. He looked over at me and then at

Kenny and I knew he was thinking that Kenny was going to be a tough out. Kenny was absolutely motionless, bat back, all concentration.

Red looked in for his sign, which had to be a fast ball. He paused. Now was the time to test those rabbit ears, I thought.

"Let's see your curve, Red," I called out.

Red's eyes flickered my way. They shouldn't have. He should have been concentrating just as much as Kenny. He breathed in, pumped and threw—not a fast ball but a change-up. His first of the game. The coiled spring that was Kenny Banks waited and waited and waited and then it sprung. His bat lashed out at the ball and sent it screaming over the shortstop's head and into left field. Solid hit. First hit for us. Red could be distracted. Kenny made a big turn at first, daring the left fielder to throw, but the kid smartly lobbed it in to second.

Or was it so smart? Did Kenny see the lob? Did he know that at some future time he might be able to lull that left fielder with a bluff and then blast off for second ahead of that automatic lob throw? See it and store it away and use it at the right time.

"I think you got to Red," Stu Abels whispered to me. "He's annoyed with himself."

Red was annoyed with himself for departing from his bread and butter pitch and trying to show me he could do something fancy, too. He glanced at me. I grinned at him but he didn't grin back. He frowned and fiddled with his cap, trying to get his concentration back as our left fielder, Bob Gordon, stepped in.

Bob batted lefty. Their third baseman moved way in, looking for the bunt. I didn't think Jim had called for a bunt. He had his cap off. Hit away. Now was the time to jump Red Kelly.

Red looked at first and then stepped onto the rubber. Kenny Banks took a long lead off first and sure enough he drew one throw and then another.

It was good. Red's mind was really divided now. Part of it was at first base, part of it was at home plate, and when I called out to him quietly, in a lull in the noise: "This is the inning, Red," part of it was focused on me.

All of this could only help Bob Gordon at bat.

Red pitched . . . wide. Kenny bluffed a steal. The catcher fooled us by firing to first and he almost picked Kenny off. He had to dive back in headfirst.

"Don't get picked off, Kenny," Warren Miller called out, as though Kenny had wanted to get picked off. That's one of the things I always loved about baseball, guys advising you on the obvious. It was more to reassure themselves.

Red looked over his shoulder at Kenny who wasn't taking such a long lead now. He threw to the plate. Bob Gordon topped the ball, a kind of swinging bunt, a squibbler, hard to field, spinning . . . Who had it? Third baseman? Pitcher? They were charging it from different directions. They were on a collision course. I instinctively winced. At the last second Red Kelly yelled: "Yours," and fell flat on his face to give his third baseman a clear shot at first. The third baseman barehanded it and fired off balance to first. The throw was high. The first baseman leaped and knocked it down. Kenny kept going and steamed into third standing up. Bob Gordon was on first with a fluke hit, and best of all, Red Kelly and his third baseman were arguing about whose fault it was. The Ace coach yelled at them to settle down and play ball. Easier said than done. Red deserved better than he received on that play. Or maybe I just felt for pitchers.

Who was up now? Tip Barnett, then Stu Abels. Then me. Unless there was a double play, I would bat this inning.

"C'mon, Tip," Jim Anderson called down, "bring Kenny home."

I swung a bat and watched Jim send a signal down to Tip and then one across the diamond to Bob Gordon. I didn't know what they were. But I could guess he was telling Bob to go on the first pitch. Draw a throw to second and Kenny will go on it.

Although Tip looked steady as a rock at the plate— most catchers do—he broke his wrists upward, as most stubby catchers do. Why that is I'll never know. Maybe it's because they throw out of a crouch, always throwing upward.

Red Kelly looked at Kenny who was coming down the line a little, and then he fired hard to the plate. Bob Gordon was running. The catcher let him go. Now there were Dairies on second and third, no one out.

"This is the inning, Red," I called out, and once again Red looked at me. I made a thumbs-up gesture to him, but he looked away. Good. I was still on his mind. Let's see if it could help Tip.

Tip had taken a strike. Now he dug in. He swung from the end of the bat. If I had been Red Kelly I'd have fed Tip a slow curve. But Red didn't have a slow curve. Red had a hard fast ball. If Tip caught hold of one he could pole it out of the park. With a swing like Tip's it was either feast or famine.

It turned out to be famine. Tip popped it up to Red Kelly, and that brought up Stu Abels.

Red looked over at me and winked. He felt better. Abels was no threat. He swung with a choked bat and didn't look happy to be at bat. He was one of those fidgety batters, too, always moving his feet in the box, looking around the diamond. You can't hit a ball well if you don't set your feet, but Stu Abels wouldn't set his feet. He was Red's meat. The fast ball blew by him three times straight. Stu didn't take his bat off his shoulder. He was too smart to swing at a ball he couldn't see. Too smart or too dumb.

"Up to you, Paul," Monk croaked from the first base coaching box.

"Win your own game, Paul," Warren Miller called out.

"Show them pitchers can hit, Paul," Jim Anderson called down to me.

I looked at him. "Hit away. No signals. Just hit away."

There hadn't been time for him and me to go over all the batting signals. I didn't need any. Runners on second and third, two out. My job was to get them in.

I tossed away the lead doughnut and stepped in. I hadn't swung at a ball in a year, even in practice. Kelly looked gigantic on the mound. He was grinning at me. Now I couldn't fuss him from the bench. Now he had me just where he wanted me.

I moved my hands up on the bat. I wasn't a great hitter in California or Texas and didn't expect to be in Michigan either, but I had a good eye and if Red grooved one I might be able to get wood on it.

Red went to a full motion. Kenny came down the line and held up. The pitch was a fast ball inside. I jumped back. Was he dusting me off? Boy, that was the last thing I needed—to get hit with a baseball.

Red was grinning at me. I grinned back to let him know I wasn't scared, which wasn't quite true. Also, I was trying to let him know that two could play at that game, and I could throw harder than he.

Red bore down. He'd forgotten about the base runners. I was the enemy. He was going to a full windup. This would be a good time for Jim to send Kenny Banks all the way in, but I guess Jim wasn't taking any chances this early in the game.

Red pumped, kicked, and came down, blinding fast. I held my bat across the plate. The ball hit it. The bat bounced in my hands. The ball was on the ground, skipping into the hole between third and short.

The guys were shrieking: "Run, Paul, run."

I had a hard time getting started. I hadn't run in a long time. I dug for first. The first baseman was getting set for the throw. It would be close, and then I saw it was going to be even closer because the first baseman was shifting his feet, lunging my way. The throw was coming in off target, to the home plate side of first. Three bodies were arriving at the same place at the same time: the ball, the first baseman, and me. Jackass, I thought, you're supposed to avoid collisions, not run into them.

I was thinking that when we hit together. The ball was up in the air off his glove, but so was I. I cartwheeled over him and came down hard on my side.

The ball was rolling behind first. Kenny Banks had scored, Bob Gordon was rounding third and heading home. The first baseman was chasing the ball. I had to reach first or no runs would score. Move . . . move!

But I couldn't get myself up.

Then crawl, darn you, Paul Mather, crawl!

I crawled, inch by inch, foot by foot. I heard the yelling and the screaming, and I knew he was running back to me with the ball. Finally I lunged and fell forward and touched first base with my right hand before he stepped on the bag.

"Safe," the bases ump shouted.

"Time," someone yelled.

It was Monk. He was bending over me, peering into my face. "Paul, Paul, are you all right?"

Jim Anderson was running over. Adults were coming across the diamond toward me, and from where I lay, I could see at least one adult that wasn't supposed to be here. He wasn't even supposed to know I was here.

"Monk," I whispered, "get me up quick."

Monk pulled me up, but I couldn't stand on my own. I held onto him.

"Where does it hurt, Paul?" Monk asked.

"I'm OK."

And then a familiar hand took my arm and a familiar voice, angrier than I had ever heard it before in my life, said, "Paul, you fool! You little fool!"

My father was so angry he couldn't talk. He choked on his words.

"I'm glad you're here, Mr. Mather," I heard Jim Anderson say. "I think Paul's all right. He's a little shaken up, but—"

"He's not all right," Dad said angrily. "He shouldn't be playing baseball. He's not well at all."

"But, sir, you signed his entry card."

"I signed nothing of the sort."

"But—"

Dad led me off to the side and I sat down. The game had stopped. Everyone was standing around talking. The Ace coach was there and I heard him say: "Is there something wrong with your new boy's entry card, Jim?"

I didn't hear Jim's answer. I didn't want to hear it. I looked up at my father.

"I'm sorry, Dad."

"Why, Paul? Why did you do it?"

"I had to."

Dad shook his head. Around us, confusion reigned.

12 THE SHORT SEASON

Two ARGUMENTS were going on at once.

At home plate, the Ace coach was claiming a forfeit victory. "You've been playing with an unregistered player, Jim. Check Section 21 of the rule book."

"Doug, if you'll just look at this kid's entry card, you'll agree you would have accepted it too."

"I'll only agree it's tough luck for you."

The other argument was taking place near our bench and it was a one-way screaming session between the Wilson Dairy team and Monk Lawler.

"You knew he forged his father's name, Lawler, why didn't you say something?"

"You had to know. He changed his clothes at your house."

"Those two guys were whispering together in the truck."

"If we lose this game on a forfeit, it's your fault."

"Why'd you let him do it?"

"You could have stopped it."

"Listen, guys," Monk began.

But they wouldn't listen to him. They went on yelling.

Dad and I, sitting in the grass near first base, were the only quiet people there. Dad was waiting for me to get my strength back to take me away. I didn't want to go, not till I helped Monk. As I sat there listening to the yelling and the shrieking I knew there was one thing we could do. The only hitch was that my father had to do it. I needed his co-operation, and he was still pretty mad at me.

"Dad," I said, "before we go . . ."

"We're going *now*, Paul. Dr. Kinsella is expecting us at the hospital."

"The hospital? Dad, I'm OK. That bump at first wasn't anything."

"I hope it wasn't, Paul. But Dr. Kinsella said to bring you in. I called him before I left the house."

That was how my father operated. Carefully, thoughtfully.

"How did you know where we were playing?"

"We called Mrs. Anderson."

"And I suppose you knew I was playing from Larry."

"That's right. And I don't want you to be angry with him. He was afraid to tell us. I'm glad he did. How do you feel now? Can you get up?"

"Of course I can get up. I feel fine. I could go on pitching right now."

Dad smiled. He didn't want to smile, but he did. "Come on now, give me your arm."

"I can do it alone."

"Can I help?" It was Jim Anderson, standing there. Neither of us had seen him come over.

"I think we can manage, thank you," Dad said coldly.

"Is Paul all right?"

"We won't know that till I get him to the hospital. Give me your arm, son."

"Dad, I'm all right. I can walk myself."

Before Dad could make a move, I got up and took a couple of steps. I swayed. Everything started to go round and round. They caught me before I could fall.

"Easy, son."

"I'll be OK in a second."

I breathed in. "Mr. Anderson, I'm sorry. I didn't think I'd get us in trouble. But if my dad'll sign the entry blank right now, then I'd really be a member of the league and the team. Isn't that right?"

Jim thought about it a moment and then shook his head. "You'd be a member of the team now, but not when we started the game and not when you were striking out all their boys and not when you knocked in the two runs. You did an awful lot of damage to Ace Appliance when you were an illegal member of our team. But that's not important now. The important thing is to get you better again. Let me give you a hand, Mr. Mather."

"Why don't you just try it, Jim? What do you have to lose? My dad'll sign it, won't you, Dad?"

Dad didn't want to sign anything. He wanted to get me out of there as quickly as possible.

Jim, on the other hand, was a coach. He looked from me to my father. "Well, it probably *is* worth a try."

Dad shrugged. "Give me the card."

Jim fished the card out of his pocket again. It was really crumpled now. An awful lot of hands had been holding it the last few minutes.

"Do you have a pen?"

"Right here, sir."

"Use my back to write on, Dad."

Holding onto Jim, I turned around and against my back I felt Dad cross out the forgery and write his own name over it. I felt useful to the team again, just standing there. The three of us made an unusual sight and in no time at all we had attracted a crowd of Dairy players.

"What's going on?" Warren Miller asked.

"My dad just signed for real."

"Hey, did you guys hear that? Paul's dad signed for real."

"That means we can go on with the game."

"Hey, batter up."

"Who's up?"

"Who bats after Mather?"

"Sloan, Miller, Lawler, Hakken . . ."

"How many outs?"

"Nobody's out."

"Two outs, dummy."

"I was only trying."

"2-0. Let's get some more runs."

"Hold on, boys," Jim Anderson said. "Don't get your hopes up like that. This," he said, holding up the entry card, "is only half the battle. Now I've got to fight out the rest of it. It's up to Mr. Parker, their coach. Remember now, Paul wasn't a member of this team when we started the game."

"Oh, nuts."

"Let's go fight the other battle, Jim," Tip Barnett said, and he and the others followed Jim back to home plate where the Ace coach and the Ace team and the umps were still discussing the unusual situation.

"Paul," Dad said quietly, "I think this is a good time to leave."

"I want to find out what happens."

"We can call Jim Anderson later."

I ignored Dad and took a couple of steps toward home plate. I almost lost my balance. Dad grabbed me.

"Paul."

"That pitching took more out of me than I thought. Boy, am I ever out of shape."

Dad didn't answer. He just held me. I heard the Ace coach laugh. "Sorry, Jim, but it's a little late for that now, don't you think? Your illegal player was responsible for the two runs you've got, not to mention getting my boys out in the first two innings."

"I'd be willing to start the game over, Doug."

"Sorry, Jim, but we can't do that. That's not baseball. There's no provision in the rule book for starting a game over after two innings are played. Is there, ump?"

"Don't think so, Mr. Parker."

"It's tough, but I'm afraid we've got you on a forfeit, Jim. I don't like to win a game this way. On the other hand, your coming in with a ringer from California was no way to play either. I don't even know that he's twelve years old."

"He's in our class at school," Monk said.

"He could have been left back, Monk," the Ace coach said. "When something like this happens, all bets are off. You've got to go by the rule book. That's all you've got."

"Nuts," Monk said, "you just want to win any way you can."

"Easy, Monk," Jim cautioned. "Doug, I know we don't have a legal leg to stand on, but baseball is what this program is all about. Giving kids a chance to play ball."

The Ace coach grinned. "Oh, I'm willing to play a game with your boys, Jim. But not for the record. For the record, your team has forfeited."

"Let's go," I whispered to Dad.

I felt sick. Heartsick.

As Dad and I left the diamond, everyone was still standing around talking, except the umps. They were picking up the bases.

13 NO PEP TALKS FOR THIS PATIENT

THAT WAS over a month ago. Since then I've been in the hospital. Tom Kinsella said my coming to the hospital and staying had nothing to do with the collision at first base.

"The tests here and in California indicated your condition was becoming unstable anyway."

"What's that mean?"

"Your system was manufacturing too many white blood cells."

"You mean, no matter what I did, my disease was coming back."

"That's right."

"Would you have given me permission to play?"

"Probably not."

"Then I'm glad I did what I did."

"Got your team a forfeit?"

"No, pitched two innings."

He smiled. "Spoken like a true pitcher. I've never known a pitcher who didn't think the whole world revolved around him."

"What position did you play?"

"Catcher."

"I guess I can expect a lot of pep talks from you then."

He laughed. "Only when you need them, sport, which may not be often."

He was like no doctor I'd ever had before. He was young, relaxed, and informal. Sometimes he'd come in right after I'd had the medication, sit down in the visitor's chair, put his feet up on my bed, and talk. It took me a while to realize the timing of those visits was not accidental.

Once he held my head while I threw up and twice he helped Brophy and an orderly clean up. Afterward, when I was feeling better, he'd sit and tell me how he threw a guy out at second once only the guy was stealing third at the time.

"For a long time they called me Wrong Base Kinsella."

He knew how to break bad news better than any doctor I ever had.

"Sport, I got a better medicine for you to take."

"What's wrong with the old one?"

"This has got more fizz in it. You'll like it better."

It was just as bad, as we both knew it would be.

He was as honest with me as a doctor could be.

I'd overheard two orderlies in the hall saying that kids

with leukemia only got three chances. The third time they got it they were out.

"Is that true, Tom?"

"Not always."

"Because I had it in Texas and got it back again in California and now I've got it here."

"You may have it ten times, sport, for all we really know about it."

"If it *were* true, would you tell me?"

"Sure."

"Do you ever lie to me, Tom?"

His eyes crinkled. "If I said yes, I could be lying about that, too, couldn't I?"

He came by one afternoon when my folks and Larry were visiting. Larry had never seen Tom juggle, so Tom put on the act for him, at my request. My mother was amused, my father was puzzled, Larry was popeyed.

"Where'd you learn to do that, Dr. Kinsella?" the Punk asked.

"In medical school," Tom said, "where else?"

I saw Tom three or four times a day. He came in early in the morning after the temperature-taking and the blood samples. He read my reports.

"How'm I doing?" I'd ask him.

"You're holding your own."

"I want to be playing ball this summer."

"So do I."

"You're too old to play."

"I can catch anything you can throw, Mather," he said, and replaced the clipboard.

"Wait till I get well."

"I will."

I wasn't getting well, though, and we both knew it. They gave me a blood transfusion, and I felt better for a while. But I was losing weight. I could see it in Mom's eyes. She looked shocked, even though she tried to cover it up by talking about other things. Dad was a better actor than Mom. Larry's solution was not to look at me at all. He'd go right to my window and look out and say what a terrific view I had and how you could see the railroad tracks and the river.

Tom was the only one I could talk to. And during a really bad time when he'd changed the medication again and I ached and burned and itched and was crying that I didn't want to take any more medicine, he came in and gave me a shot and sat with me.

"Why me, Tom? Why me?"

"I don't know, Paul. But I'm going to find out someday. A lot of people are working both day and night on it. You know, I became a children's doctor because it's hopeful. When you cure a kid you cure him for a long time. I specialized in blood diseases because a lot of work has to be done there, especially with kids. You're not alone, Paul. Neither am I. There's a lot of us in this together and sooner or later we're going to pull through."

"Make it sooner, Tom."

"I will, sport."

Just the same he looked worried when I said my plan was to get back to the baseball diamond this summer.

"You don't think I'm going to make it, do you?" I challenged him.

"It won't be easy, Paul."

"But it's possible, isn't it?"

"Anything's possible."

"What would happen if you cut down my extra dosage?"

"You'd get worse."

"I'm getting worse now."

"Not really."

"Yes, I am. I know I am."

"Some days you win a little, some days you lose."

"You're not being honest with me."

"Yes, I am."

"No, you're not. You're as bad as my folks and the Punk. They don't think I'm going to make it. I can see it in their eyes. They're scared. But I'm going to make it, Tom."

"I think you will too, Paul."

"No, you don't. You're only saying that because you have to, as a doctor."

"I don't have to say anything as a doctor."

"Sure you do."

"No, I don't."

"Do you think I'll be back for that second game against Ace Appliance? Answer yes or no."

He hesitated. "No."

"But I will. I know I will."

He didn't say anything. What could he say?

Another time, after a rough night . . .

"Tom, there's a way you can help me."

"How's that, sport?"

"Cut down my extra dosage. It's killing me."

"That won't get you back in uniform, sport."

"Yes, it will, if you give me something for the pain."

"Now what have you been overhearing in the hall?"

"I heard some nurses say some kid was getting pain-killer and he's acting better. I want some pain-killer, Tom."

"Sport, when people get pain-killer they're doing worse, not better. All they were saying was that it was easier to take care of Toddy now. You've got to stop listening to people who talk in the halls."

"Will you cut down on my medicine, then?"

"You could go to jail, Paul."

"What for?"

"Practicing medicine without a license."

"Where do you think I am now?"

"So that's what you think of this place, do you?"

Over and over it was the old question again. It haunted us both. Me personally, and him medically.

"Why do I have to be sick, Tom?"

"You know I don't know, sport. All I do know is that time is on our side."

It always came down to "time"—buying time with drugs, transfusions, waiting for new cures to come out of the laboratories.

And then late one night . . . I don't know what he was doing in the hospital at that hour or even if he was there. I mean, I don't know whether I dreamed the whole thing or not, but it was just a few days before the date I had set to be out of the hospital on—August first. I'd taken the extra dosage and worn the rubber cap and been miserable, unable to eat, and that night I had pain. I must have cried out. Brophy was there, and so was Tom. And he gave me a shot that made the pain go away. I can remember asking him at one point if I was going to die. He said: "Everyone has to die sometime, sport."

"But I don't want to die, Tom. Not yet."

122

"You're not going to die for a long time, sport. At least not till I learn to juggle four balls. And that's going to take me a long, long time."

He could make a joke that wasn't really funny but we'd both try to laugh to get out of where we were.

But then, another time, when I wasn't hurting and he'd come in to check me over, he sat down and we talked about death. I asked him if he thought science would ever get to the point where people would be able to live forever, and he said he didn't think so and hoped they wouldn't have to. Because you got old and feeble and at a certain point it was just hard work breathing. And not worth it.

I asked him if he was afraid of dying himself.

He thought about it. "I guess I would be, sport." And then he looked at me. "How about you?"

Suddenly we weren't doctor and patient, but two friends, even though he was thirty-something and I was twelve. And I knew then that I knew things he didn't know. I knew them because I had death inside me, I could feel it sometimes hard as a rock and sometimes soft and running crazy through my veins. I knew it first-hand; he only knew it from books and . . . from me.

"Yes," I said, "I'm scared. Even when I'm so nauseous I wish I were dead, I'm still scared of dying."

"That's interesting," Tom said, as if I'd really told him something.

Tom came in while the whole Dairy team was visiting me.

"So this is the infamous Wilson Dairy team," he said. "Which one's Monk Lawler?"

"Me," Monk said in that old croaky voice of his.

"How about letting me examine your voice box, son," Tom said, with a straight face.

"Keep away," Monk said, backing off, "you just work on getting Paul better."

"Paul Mather? You really need him on the team?"

"We won't make the playoffs unless he gets back," Stu Abels said. "And we got to beat Ace to make the playoffs."

"Well, I'll see what I can do. If I think there's one thing that's important in life, it's seeing that Wilson Dairy makes the playoffs."

They all laughed, but no one said anything more about me coming back because nobody really knew what to expect.

Mom came afternoons and knitted. She liked Tom.

"You give Paul a lot of time, Dr. Kinsella," Mom said to him.

"I like Paul."

"I'm sure you like all your patients, Doctor."

"That's true. But I do like Paul a lot."

"He likes me for my disease, Mom. He wouldn't like me if I wasn't sick."

Tom laughed. "That's not true. When you get better I'm going to catch you and maybe show you a few things about throwing a baseball."

"Maybe I'll show you a few things."

"You have already," Tom said, and turned to Mom. "That's one reason I like Paul."

"I told you he liked me for my disease."

They both laughed.

Tom and my father got along carefully. Dad thought

Tom was "young." Once he started asking him about where he had trained.

The answer was that Tom had been an undergraduate at Michigan and had trained at Harvard. It set Dad back. He didn't understand how a man could be a first-rate doctor and scientist and still call people "sport" and juggle baseballs. He was even more astonished when he learned that Tom had a big grant from the government to run a research lab in addition to his clinical duties.

"It's a wonder you have any home life at all," Mom said to Tom.

"I don't," Tom said. "I've got two little girls who think I'm a stranger called Daddy."

After he left, Dad said, "I guess it keeps him loose."

"What does?" Mom asked.

"Juggling," Dad said. Mom and I laughed. The juggling bothered Dad. Geology professors never juggled baseballs.

The one who admired Tom the most was the Punk. Larry had found out that Tom had been a three-sport letterman at the university, and that one of those three sports had been basketball.

"How big were you in fourth grade?" the Punk asked him.

"Smaller than you," Tom said, which was the answer the Punk wanted to hear. To him that meant he'd grow up to be six foot two, and star in three sports, and maybe even be a terrific doctor too.

But I don't think I've really shown Tom to be a terrific doctor. For one thing I wasn't getting better. For another thing, it's hard to describe the kind of doctor he was. On TV, doctors wear masks and call for scalpels. Tom didn't do anything like that. He'd come in, go over my reports, change the prescription of my medicine, talk with me, maybe give me a shot, and talk with me some more.

He told me one of his big jobs with kids was to keep their dobbers up, not let them get discouraged. With me, it was just the opposite, though we never talked about it like that. My dobber was too far up. I was determined to be out of this hospital on August first. I was sure I would be out. My dobber was so high it scared him. He didn't think I was going to make it on August first. He didn't think I'd be back on that ball diamond. He didn't think I had a chance at all.

He was wrong.

14 RETURN OF A UNIFORM

"BROPHY, what's today?"

"July thirty-first, lad. Now, sit up—"

"That makes tomorrow August first, doesn't it?"

"I guess it does. Now let's go with the medicine, Paul. One, two, three, and down the—"

I turned my head away. "What happens on August first, Brophy?"

"You get sick because you didn't take your medicine the day before."

"No, Brophy. Wilson Dairy plays its revenge game against Ace Appliance."

"How could I forget that? Now, turn to me and—"

"Everybody's forgetting. Tom's forgotten, my folks have

forgotten. Well, I haven't forgotten. I'm going to the game, Brophy, and I need my uniform."

"Do I look like I have a baseball uniform on me, Paul?"

"That uniform's somewhere. I wore it here to the hospital. My mom says she doesn't know where it is. I want it now. I'm not going to take any medicine till I get my uniform."

"Do you want me to get Dr. Kinsella down, is that what you want, Paul?"

"I want my uniform."

"You take your medicine and I'll look for it."

"I won't take my medicine till I have it."

I glared at her and she glared at me.

"All right," she said, "I'll fetch Dr. Kinsella down here."

With that, she left. I put the pills back on the table. They weren't doing me much good anyway. What would help me most now was if they brought my uniform and let me get my revenge against Ace Appliance.

I lay there and waited for Tom to come down. He was a long time coming. Finally he came in with Brophy right behind him.

"What's this I hear, sport, about your not wanting to take your medicine?"

"That's right. I want my uniform. Tomorrow's August first. I'm going to play in that game."

Tom looked at me and then sat down in the chair next to my bed. "Sport, you won't be able to play tomorrow."

"How do you know?"

"I know."

"You don't know. You've told me lots of times you don't understand my disease. I could get completely better overnight. I heard you say that once."

128

Tom smiled. "I always thought I talked too much to you."

"Amen," Brophy said.

"So I'm not taking any medicine till I get my uniform."

"You're only hurting yourself, Paul."

"You're not helping me. I'm going to that ball game tomorrow and no one's going to stop me."

Tom turned to Brophy. "Where is that uniform, Brophy?"

"Mrs. Mather has it, Doctor."

"And she said she didn't know where it was."

"She probably doesn't," Brophy said. "We sent it to your house with some other things of yours."

"Call her and tell her to find it and bring it with her tomorrow."

"Dr. Kinsella, you don't mean to tell me—"

"Go call her, Brophy."

Brophy left the room.

"How're you going to get there, sport?"

"You'll take me."

Tom laughed. He swung the medicine tray over to me. "They don't pay me big money to take old pitchers to ball games. Chug-a-lug."

He had called me an "old pitcher." I grinned. There had been a lot of affection in that. He was an "old catcher."

"I'll arrange for something. Let's go."

I took my medicine. Pill, water, swallow; pill, water, swallow; pill, water, swallow; pill, water, swallow.

"Way to go." He took the empty cup from me.

Brophy came back in. "Mrs. Mather found the uniform but she says it's dirty."

"Tell her that's OK. It's better that way," Tom said.

129

"Maybe you'd better tell her yourself, Doctor," Brophy said.

"Maybe I'd better," Tom said, and winked at me as he left the room.

"I'm going to the game, Brophy," I said triumphantly.

"I know that," Brophy said, looking at my empty medicine tray, "and I don't approve of it at all."

"Of going to ball games?"

"No, of bribing patients to take their medicine."

"Aw, Brophy, I would have taken it anyway. I was just bluffing."

"Were you?" Brophy said angrily. She was one tough nurse.

My body's reaction to the medicine that day wasn't bad at all. I slept through a lot of it. But I didn't sleep well that night. Not because of the medicine but because I was so excited about tomorrow's game. At one point the night nurse from the desk popped into my room and asked me if I was OK.

"I'm fine."

"Why aren't you asleep?"

"I've got a big ball game tomorrow."

She thought I had a fever. She put her hand on my forehead. "You don't feel hot."

I laughed. "No, it's true. My mom's bringing my baseball uniform in tomorrow."

"Maybe I better call Dr. Kinsella."

"I'm OK. I really am."

She was unconvinced. But when I told her I'd try hard to sleep, she decided not to call up Tom.

I finally fell asleep and dreamed about all the guys I'd

ever played baseball with. In Texas, California, and here. Faces and names got mixed up and guys from my Austin, Texas, team were playing on my Palo Alto team, and guys from Palo Alto played on the Arborville team, but I pitched through it all, and we won.

It was really one of the best nights' sleep I ever had in a hospital.

In the morning I was actually hungry. I couldn't wait for the blood samples to be taken and the temperature out of the way. Tom came in while I was eating breakfast. He looked at me, smiled, and read the chart. He initialed it and hung the clipboard up again.

"Hungry?"

"Yes."

"Good. Big day today, huh?"

"Don't you know it? Are you gonna come see your patient win a ball game?"

"Paul, you know you're not going to play, don't you?"

"I don't know anything. When's my mom coming?"

"At her regular time."

"With my uniform?"

"With your uniform."

"Are you coming with us?"

"I won't be able to get away. I've got two new patients."

"Like me?"

"Like you."

"Boys or girls?"

"Both girls."

"How old are they?"

"One's four and the other's sixteen."

"Are they . . . bad?"

He nodded.

"I'll go by their rooms when I go to the game. I was pretty bad when I came in here and now I'm going to a ball game. That might cheer them up."

He smiled. "You're all right, sport."

"So are you. You're the best doctor I ever had."

"I'm not so sure about that."

"I am."

"I'm not so sure we're doing the right thing in letting you out of the hospital today."

"You are. I know you are."

"We're going to have to delay your medication till after the game."

"Good."

"You may be nauseated for a long time, sport."

"It'll be worth it."

He smiled. "I'm going to give you a shot before you go."

"A shot of what?"

"Something that'll make you feel OK, if you should start hurting at the game."

"I won't need it, Tom."

"It won't hurt."

"I don't want it."

"We'll see."

"How's my chart doing?"

"OK." He stood up. "By the way, the night nurse's report says you were hallucinating, talking crazy, during the night."

"I was just telling her about the ball game today."

Tom laughed. "I'll be by later."

"Take care."

"You too, sport."

Later that morning, Brophy opened the blinds and the sunlight poured in.

"It's a great day for a game," I said.

She ignored me.

"Don't be mad, Brophy."

"I'm not mad, Paul. I just wonder who's going to give you your medicine today."

So that was it.

"Why don't you stay around till after we get back and you give it to me?"

"I have more important things to do than give spoiled patients pills and then hold their heads for them."

"What time is it?"

"Nine thirty."

"Five more hours."

"Till what?"

"Till Mom brings my uniform. Brophy, did you tell her to bring my baseball shoes too?"

Brophy looked at me disbelievingly. "Paul Mather, you're going to drive me into a mental institution."

And she walked out.

Five long hours. I lay there and listened to the old familiar hospital sounds: carts, bells, voices, elevators stopping, opening, closing, phones ringing, TV's and radios in other rooms. I heard Brophy talking to Toddy next door. I could never hear Toddy talking back. I'd walk by Toddy's room too and show him my uniform. That might cheer him up.

Five long hours. They took forever.

Mom always came at two o'clock. Promptly at two I heard the elevator stop at our floor, and then I heard her talking to the nurses at central desk, and Brophy talking, and then Mom came down the hall.

She came in the room and she was carrying my uniform over her arm.

"You didn't wash it, did you?"

"No," she said, smiling.

"I want to put it on now."

"Paul, that's a heavy wool uniform. We won't be leaving till five. You'll suffocate in it."

"I want to put it on anyway. Did you bring my shoes?"

"What shoes?"

"My baseball shoes."

"No."

"Oh, Mom."

"You have a pair of sneakers here. You can wear them."

"Where's my glove?"

"Larry has it. He and your father will be along soon."

"What's he doing with my glove?"

"He's been taking care of it. Oiling it."

"That's good. What about my cap?"

"It's right here. And your socks and your undershirt."

"Help me put it on."

"Let's wait, Paul."

"I've waited long enough, Mom. C'mon, help me."

"I'll get Brophy."

"You and I can do it, Mom."

But we couldn't. I didn't have the strength to help her. So she got Brophy and the two of them got my hospital gown off and my uniform on.

"Where's the mirror?" I asked Brophy.

There had been a mirror in the room but it had disappeared a couple of weeks before.

"I don't remember a mirror here," Brophy said.

"There used to be one there. Could you get me one? I want to see what I look like."

"You look fine, Paul," Mom said.

"How could I? This uniform was too big for me before I got sick. I bet I look awful."

"You look all right," Brophy said flatly. "I never heard of an athlete wanting to see what he looked like in the mirror."

They wouldn't get me a mirror, but I guess I didn't need one. The mirror was in Dad's eyes when he came in and saw me in the uniform. Larry looked away faster than usual.

Nuts to them both, I thought. Nothing was going to spoil today.

"When can we leave?"

"It's only four o'clock. Your game doesn't start till five forty-five," Dad said.

"Let's go early and drive around."

Mom and Dad looked at each other.

"Anyway," Mom said, "we can't go until Dr. Kinsella gets here."

So then we waited for Dr. Kinsella. The Punk looked out the window and watched a train go by, Mom and Dad sat and talked, and I lay there in my uniform, feeling good and silly at the same time.

Finally I heard a squeaking down the hall. It wasn't a sound that would accompany Tom, but this time it did. The door opened wide and Tom came in pushing a brand-new shiny wheelchair.

"Neato," Larry said. "I get to push it."

I stared at it and Tom looked at me. Who was kidding

who? I had talked about playing in the game but I hadn't been able to even put on my own uniform without help.

They were waiting for me to put up an objection to the wheelchair. But I didn't.

"Let's go," I said.

"First, a shot," Tom said, and I didn't object to that either.

15 RETURN OF A BALL PLAYER

IT TOOK US a while to get out of the hospital. First I wanted to say hello to Toddy who was the nine-year-old boy next door. He smiled when he saw me. Ruthie, in the room next to Toddy's, was sleeping. I went to say hello to Tom's new patients but I guess the sight of me was too much for them. They just stared at me.

Then the parade started down the corridor and everyone moved aside for us: attendants, nurses, a couple of young doctors. The Punk pushed me. Mom and Dad walked on one side of me and Tom and Brophy were on the other side.

The elevators were across from the central desk, and while the elevator was on its way, everyone came around from behind the desk to get a good look at me. They wished me luck and made a big fuss.

I was relieved when the elevator came.

"You'd think they'd never seen a ball player before," Tom said with a straight face.

We all laughed.

It was more of the same in the main lobby of the hospital. People staring at us, kids looking popeyed, nurses smiling, and finally it was out the big front door and down a ramp to the car that Dad had parked in front.

Then came the tricky part. How to get me into the front seat, which was wider than the rear seat. Tom wheeled the chair up to the car and turned it sideways. Then he and Dad put their hands together, each one grabbing the other's wrist, making a chair out of their hands. They slid their chair under my thighs, and then, kind of tickling me, got it under my seat. They were bent over the sides of the chair. It couldn't have been very comfortable for either of them.

"OK, Brophy," Tom said, and Brophy pulled the wheelchair backward. It went out from under me and I was sitting on the Kinsella-Mather chair lift. They lifted me, angling me sideways into the car. It wasn't easy, but I slid in.

"Whew," Tom said.

"I hope we can find someone there to help us," Mom said.

"I'm sure we'll have lots of help there," Dad said.

"I'm sure you will, too," Tom said. "Let me break down that chair for you, Mr. Mather."

"I can get it," Dad said. He liked to figure out things. While he broke the chair down to store it in the trunk, Tom bent over to talk to me through the open door.

"I'm sorry I can't be going with you, sport."

"Don't need you," I said, grinning.

"Didn't think you did. I'd like to see what a good ball club looks like, though."

I laughed, and he laughed too.

"Listen, have a good time out there."

"I'll try."

"Don't get all excited and bust out of your chair and run out to the mound."

"If I can, I will."

He smiled. "Don't throw too many curves at people."

It was a catcher's way of telling me to behave.

"I won't."

"And come back a winner."

"I'll try."

Tom closed the door, pushing the button down first to lock it. Mom and Larry were in the back seat. Dad had got the wheelchair stowed away and he came around to the driver's seat.

"I want to thank you for all your help, Dr. Kinsella."

"That's all right. If Paul keeps eating like he did this morning we may add baseball games to his therapy."

Brophy also bent down to talk to me. "No high jinks out there, Paul." She looked past me to my father. "He's to come back here right after the game, Mr. Mather. He hasn't had today's medication yet."

"I don't see what you're so worried about, Brophy. You won't be here."

"How do you know I won't be here?"

"You're off duty by the time we get back."

"Not today I'm not. You don't think I'm going to let just anyone give you your medicine, do you?"

Tom nodded. "She means business, I'm afraid. You all better come right back after the game."

"We will," Dad said.

"Let's go," I said.

Dad started the car and we drove off with a flurry of "good lucks" following us. Tom and Brophy were standing in front of the hospital, getting smaller and smaller as we went down the circular drive.

"He's a great guy, isn't he, Paul?" the Punk said.

"Yeah," I said, but I didn't want to talk about it. I didn't want to talk about Tom or Brophy or hospitals at all. I wanted to take it all in. This was the first time I'd been out of the hospital in over a month, and it was all going by the car window so fast: the sunlight through the trees, people on the sidewalk walking, students with books under their arms, two ladies talking over a fence, two dogs chasing each other, squirrels, birds, kids on bicycles . . . everything you take for granted until it's taken away from you.

Because we were way early for the game, Dad gave us a ride around Arborville. We drove slowly around the university campus, downtown past the department stores and shops and arcades, down by the river and the railroad tracks and the canoe livery, and then doubling back up State Street with a left on Huron and then past the university women's athletic fields, and we were on the same wide street—Washtenaw Avenue—that we'd come in on that day in early June when we first came to Arborville. Dad followed the same route and I knew we were going to head for Sampson Park by way of our rented house, because he turned off Washtenaw and went down the winding tree-lined streets with the lawns and the houses set far back, left and right and then left again. Then we were in the lane and there was our house on the left with the Punk's backboard. Dad slowed down. I looked up at the windows of the room the Punk and I shared.

"Let's go," I said, meaning: Let's speed up.

Dad stepped on the gas. We drove up to Ferdon, crossed Ferdon where the Punk had spotted me in the truck, and we went down Granger to Baldwin, and then it was like it always was near a park with baseball diamonds in it: We could hear the ball players before we could see them.

Then I saw them, and they saw me.

"There's Paul."

"Where?"

"You're kidding."

"In the car. It's Paul. Paul Mather."

"Hey, it *is* Mather."

"He's in uniform."

"Paul's gonna play."

"Jim. Paul's back. Paul Mather's back."

They came running, yelling, jumping: Monk and Tip and Stu Abels, and Cliff Borton and Kenny Banks and Jim Hakken and Warren Miller and Bob Gordon, and Ted Sloan, who was going to play shortstop, and Jim Anderson was coming after them. When they got to the car they stopped and were suddenly silent. Dad had taken the wheelchair out of the trunk and was opening it up. I think they realized then, for the first time, where I'd be during the game.

They stood there silently and then Jim Anderson pushed his way through them. "Paul," he said, "it's good to see you. How're you doing?"

"Fine."

"We're glad you could make it back. Can I give you a hand with that, Mr. Mather?"

"I've got the chair all right," Dad said, "but if you could give me a hand or, better still, two hands, we'll get Paul into it."

Dad and Jim then made the same hand chair lift that Dad and Tom had made. I slid onto their hands and they lifted me onto the wheelchair.

It was awkward, all the guys standing in a circle, watching me. Finally Monk spat, and said: "That's a pretty cool chair, Mather. You got a driver's permit for it?"

It broke the ice. They giggled. I laughed too.

"Hey, let me push it," Warren Miller said.

"No," the Punk said, "I push it."

For a second I thought the Punk and Warren Miller were going to have a fight about who would push me.

"Let my brother push it," I said.

The Punk pushed me proudly toward our bench which was on the first base side of the diamond. We were the visiting team this time. All our fans stood up to say hello though Mr. Lawler was the only one I recognized.

The Punk pushed me to the end of the bench and he put the brake on there. Except for the big wheels and the high back to the chair, you might have thought I was sitting on the bench with the rest of the team.

The guys followed us over and talked about what a great chair it was, and how it had reverse and forward and brakes on it. Then someone said, "Here comes the Ace team."

We looked up. Sure enough, the whole Ace team led by Red Kelly was coming over to say hello to me. What a way to start a revenge game. It was embarrassing. They wanted to shake hands with me and Red was first there.

"How're you doing, Mather?"

"OK. How're you doing?"

"OK. Can you pitch from that thing?"

"No."

"That's good," he said.

I shook hands with him and with four or five more guys and my arm started to feel pretty weak. The Punk stopped the whole thing.

"Just say hello," he announced, "my brother's tired."

I looked at my little brother with surprise. He didn't sound like a punk anymore. He was quietly taking charge of a lot of older guys. Larry winked at me.

So I said hello to the rest of the Ace team and even to Mr. Parker, their coach. It turned out I wasn't mad at him the way I thought I would be. He looked a little embarrassed, as well he might be, getting that cheap forfeit victory over us the last time.

"We're gonna beat you today, Coach," I said.

He laughed uneasily, wished me luck, and took off.

That took care of Ace Appliance. Our guys were warming up near me. Balls were flying back and forth.

"Where's my glove?" I asked Larry.

"Mom's got it. You're not going to throw, are you?"

"No. But something may come my way."

"I'll get it for you."

Cliff Borton, throwing near me, said: "We're gonna win this one for you, Paul."

"You darn well better."

"You got any ideas how we can get to Red?" Kenny Banks asked me.

"Not yet. If I do, I'll let you know."

Kenny was being polite, I think, but I was serious. This was my revenge game, not theirs. It was thanks to me they'd lost the last game to Ace. Now it was my job to help these guys win.

I watched our guys warm up. Every now and then they'd look at me, as if they couldn't get me off their minds. Forget about me, I growled softly. I'm on your side.

Across the field, the Ace kids warmed up, and they too would look at me every so often. Including Red, who was throwing to his catcher. There was something about that, something about Red, a weakness he had as a pitcher. I'd noticed it in the last game, but what was it exactly? I couldn't remember what it was.

Maybe it would come back to me after the game started.

16 WINNER IN A WHEELCHAIR

"PLAY BALL," the ump called out. "Batter up."

"Here we go, big Warren."

"Give it a ride, Warren."

"He's no stick, Red."

"Blow it by him, big Red."

"Are you cold, Paul?"

"No, Dad."

"Mom and I will be sitting over there. If you need anything—"

"Hey, pitcher, pitcher, pitcher."

"Hey, batter, batter, batter . . ."

It was music to my ears, all of it. I sat there, glove on my
lap, and watched big Red Kelly go into his windup.

He fired down the slot and Warren watched it go by, waist high, for a strike.

"OK, that's his pitch for the day, Warren."

"The harder they come in, the harder they go out," Jim Anderson called down.

Warren Miller stepped out of the batter's box and rubbed some dirt on his hands. He looked down at Jim, nodded, and stepped in again. Red grinned at him. Red looked confident. He poured the fast ball through there again and Warren, swinging behind the ball, ticked it foul.

"Way ahead of him, Red."

Warren stepped out of the box to pull himself together. Now he'd have to guard the plate, swing at anything close. Now Red ought to waste one if he was a real pitcher. Red pumped, kicked, and fired another one down the middle. Warren took his cut and missed it by a mile. Strike three.

It was a dumb pitch by Red, I thought. But then he did an even dumber thing. While his infield was whooping it up, throwing it around, he took a good look at me to make sure I'd seen what he'd just done.

And when he looked at me like that, I remembered then what his weakness had been in that first game. He had rabbit ears. He heard everything, and he liked to look around. Especially at me. I was the opposing pitcher then and he had made a personal duel out of it.

Red could be distracted with a few choice remarks, but I had to wait till the right time. I didn't have the strength for full-time bench jockeying. I wouldn't be able to shout over my teammates' shouts. I'd have to wait for the right moment and the right moment had to be a quiet one.

So I sat and watched while Red got the side out one, two, three. After striking out Warren, he got Monk on an easy grounder to second and then Jim Hakken, getting around late on the fast ball, popped it up to first.

Red grinned at me as he left the mound. Good. One way or another, he was still pitching against me.

Jim Anderson sat down alongside me.

"He's fast today."

"We'll get to him."

"He's eligible to pitch the whole game. I've never seen him get tired yet. This is for a playoff spot so I guess they'll let him go the whole way. Come in a little, Kenny."

Kenny Banks was playing too deep at third. Jim Hakken wasn't too fast and Kenny was worried they'd get around him and send a shot at him on third. Jim Anderson was worried about bunts, though. Hakken threw a lot of low pitches that were easy to bunt. On the other hand, he was a quick fielder and I didn't think they'd get too far bunting on him. What Jim lacked in the way of a strong arm he made up in courage and canniness. He had poise, too, and he believed in himself. Anything they got off him, they'd earn.

Their first batter bounced a high chopper down the third base line. It was good Kenny had moved in. He waited for it to come down, and then fired it sidearm across to Cliff Borton for a close out.

"Way to fire, Kenny," Jim said.

That play picked us up after Red had set us down. We whipped it around the infield. Jim Hakken tugged on his cap and took a sign from Tip Barnett.

He pitched a ball and a strike and then he speared a line drive hit right at his head. That made two outs. They'd hit Jim all right. We'd have to be airtight behind him.

Red Kelly batted third. And as he came up to the plate,

he looked at me to see if I was watching. I was tempted to shout at him, but I held up. The time to shout was when he was pitching, not batting.

Red stepped into Jim's first pitch and flied out to Stu Abels in right field and we were up again.

I waited through the second inning and the third inning for the right moment to get to Red, but we never mounted any sort of a threat. It was always a quick one, two, three. Red kept looking my way to see if I was still admiring him, and that, at least, was good.

For their part, Ace Appliance hit Jim Hakken hard, but clutch fielding by Kenny Banks and Monk Lawler and Jim himself kept the goose eggs on the scoreboard for them too.

So it was 0-0 when the fourth inning rolled around. I was getting anxious.

Monk Lawler was at bat. He looked down at Jim Anderson, and then he glanced at me. Every now and then the guys on our team would look at me, but up to now I had ignored them. This time I didn't. I cupped my hands to my mouth and shouted: "Don't look at me, Monk. Look at Red Kelly."

It was the first time I'd spoken in the game. It shook up Monk, but it shook Red Kelly up even more. He gave me a long look, and when he finally got around to pitching, he grooved one. Monk stepped into it and banged a shot down the left field line. It got him a double standing up.

That woke up our bench. It was like someone had pulled the plug. They all yelled then. I was silent. I couldn't yell over their noise.

Jim Hakken batting third took a quick strike from Red who was bearing down. The strike quieted our bench. I took advantage of it. I cupped my hands and shouted: "Hey, Red, I can pitch better than you any day."

It rattled Red. But bench jockeying is a part of baseball. Red stared at me; he stared at my wheelchair.

"Forget about him," Mr. Parker, his coach, yelled.

"I've got my eye on you, Red," I shouted.

"Work on the batter," Mr. Parker shouted.

"I'm watching you, big Red."

Red forced himself to look at the batter. Forgetting he had a man on second, he went into a windup. Monk promptly stole third. Red then threw four straight balls to Jim Hakken and we had men on first and third. Mr. Parker called time and went out to talk to Red. My dad came over to talk with me.

"Paul, you shouldn't be shouting like that."

"I'm all right, Dad."

"He's got Red confused, Mr. Mather," Stu Abels said.

"Take it easy, Paul."

"I will, Dad."

Mr. Parker went back to his bench. Dad went back to where he and Mom were sitting. Cliff Borton stepped in.

Red looked over at me. He just couldn't help it.

I grinned at him. "How're you doing, Red?" I called out.

"Forget about Mather," Mr. Parker yelled angrily. "Work on the batter."

Easier said than done. I was inside Red and we both knew it. He went into his windup and Jim stole second. Red threw into the dirt. Monk bluffed going home and came back.

"Red, Red," I said, "don't wind up."

He looked at me and shook his head.

Monk went down the line at third.

"He's going, Red," I called out.

Red glanced at Monk as he was throwing. He threw a half-hearted fast ball. It was way inside, but Cliff Borton couldn't resist the fatness of it. He put his foot in the bucket and pulled the ball over the third baseman's head, a screaming liner that stayed fair.

Oh, the screaming and yelling. Monk scored. Jim scored. Cliff chugged into third, Jim Anderson held him up, the ball was coming to the shortstop, it bounced off his leg. Jim sent Cliff in and he scored too, sliding across the plate in a cloud of dust and triumph.

Everyone on the team ran to meet him and pound his back.

I sat back in my chair, exhausted. It was as though I'd hit that ball and run those bases and slid that slide. I was out of it now. Too much yelling, too much emotion. I closed my eyes.

"Paul," an old familiar voice croaked.

I opened my eyes. Monk was squatting in front of me.

"Paul, man," he said, "you weren't even in the game and you got to Red before we did. You're a winner, man."

I smiled. Nodded. I was too tired to talk, even quietly. Everything had been drained out of me. I was through for the game.

The guys got two more runs off Red that inning. Tip Barnett, with that big upward swing, finally got his long hit, driving in Kenny Banks who'd walked ahead of him. Mr. Parker gave up and took Red out. The new pitcher was all business and nothing would distract him. He got the side out. But the damage was done. Five big runs. A fat enough lead for a crafty battler like Jim Hakken. When Monk came in in the fifth with his nothing ball, they got two runs but that was all. We won 5-2, and from the way the guys were jumping up and down and throwing their caps in the air and hugging each other, I guess it put us in the playoffs.

It took a few minutes for the Ace kids to get themselves together. Then they came over and shook hands with the Dairies, including me. A couple of them mumbled "Good game" to me, but most of them just sort of looked away as they shook hands. It was a tough game for them to lose.

Red Kelly came up to me. We shook hands.

"You're tough, Mather."

"So're you, Red."

He smiled ruefully. "Not tough enough. Take care. I'm gonna beat you next year."

"Never."

He faked a light punch at my chin and then went with the rest of his team to their bench.

"Red's all right," Monk said. "But you're a winner, Paul."

"And in a wheelchair," Stu Abels said. "Hey, guys, let's get some Dairy Queens. Paul, are you coming?"

I shook my head.

"Can he come with us, Mr. Mather?" Tip asked.

"I'm afraid not," Dad said.

"You got to come to the next game, Paul," Warren Miller said.

"We can't win without you, man," Cliff said.

"Good game, Paul," Monk said.

They said a lot more things like that and then they took

off in Jim Anderson's pickup truck for the Dairy Queen. They were happy, yelling and pounding the side of the truck.

We took off for the hospital. Not yelling, not pounding anything, but happy, too.

17 HANG TOUGH, PAUL MATHER

"WELL, DID YOU WIN?" Brophy asked, as Larry wheeled me into the room.

"Did they ever win?" Larry said excitedly. "And you know who won it for them? Paul did. From his wheelchair too!"

And, boasting as usual, the Punk told Brophy what happened.

"Well, how about that," Brophy said, moving the chair over to the side of the bed. "I always said baseball was a very brainy sport. Now if you'll lend me a hand here, Mr. Mather . . ."

Together, Dad and Brophy eased me onto the bed.

"There," Brophy said. "From the looks of you I'd say you were right in the game. Tired?"

I nodded.

"Well, a good night's sleep will fix you up fine. Say good-bye to your folks now. Tomorrow you can all relive the big baseball game."

Mom kissed me good-bye, Dad rubbed my head. My brother grinned at me. "Good game, Paul. Really, a good game."

"Thanks . . . Larry," I said.

They left.

"Where's Tom?" I asked.

"He's with his new patients. You just relax. He'll be by soon. So you won a ball game. Well, I'm proud of you. I really am. Lean over."

She took off my baseball cap and put on my tight rubber cap. Old Brophy didn't waste any time. She'd stayed on duty just to be here. She'd make a pretty good ball club manager, I thought.

For once I didn't protest the pills. I was too tired. I just took them down, one, two, three, four.

Then I lay back.

"Hold on. What do you think you're doing? Sit up now, Paul. We've got to get that uniform off you."

"Not yet, Brophy," I begged.

"What do you mean, not yet? You can't sleep in that thing. It's against hospital regulations."

"Just leave it on a little while longer, please."

Brophy hesitated. Then she smiled. "All right, but just a little while. Lie down. Dr. Kinsella will be in soon and you can tell him all about it. How do you feel now?"

"Fine."

"Good. Maybe you'll sleep through the reaction."

Maybe I would. I was tired enough. I didn't think anything could wake me up. I felt as drained of energy as though I'd pitched nine hard innings. Even now, in the old hospital bed again, it was hard for me to believe where I had been today: out in the real world, in the sunlight, under trees, on grass, guys shouting, hitting, running. . . .

I closed my eyes so I could see it all again. Monk and Red Kelly and Cliff Borton pulling that inside pitch and Tip's big upward swing and Jim Hakken pitching craftily to the corners and Cliff chugging around those bases with everyone up and screaming.

Then the guys from my California team came into the game and the kids I'd grown up with in Texas. They were all there, playing in the same game, on the same team, my team.

I fell asleep in my uniform with that crazy beautiful dream running through my head.

The nausea woke me up.

"Tom!"

"I'm right here, sport."

"I feel bad, Tom."

"I know, sport. You had a big day."

The night lamp was on. Tom took a needle from the table. I was too sick, too aching to object. "Brophy says you won it for them." He shot me in the arm. "What was the score, sport?"

"5-2."

He put the needle down and patted my arm. "And you won it. From a wheelchair too." He unbuttoned my uniform shirt. The night nurse was there. She helped him. Together they took off my shirt and my undershirt and then my pants.

"Tom . . ." I whispered.

"What is it, sport?"

"Keep the uniform around."

"We will, sport. It'll stay right here in the room."

"I'm hanging it right here in the closet, Paul," the night nurse said.

Tom put the hospital gown around me.

"You'll sleep now, Paul. In the morning I want to hear all about it, blow by blow."

"Tom . . ."

"Yes, sport?"

"Thanks for letting me out."

"You got yourself out, Paul. You fooled us all."

We were both silent.

"Good night, Tom."

"Good night, sport. Hang tough."

"I will."

And that's where I am now. Or, I should say, *we* are now. Tom and me. We're hanging tough. It's not easy. There's pain, and Tom says lots more to come. But Tom also says time is on my side. Time and medicine and research and my own battling instincts. If anyone can make it, he says, I can. Even Brophy, who doesn't go along with many things, goes along with that. She's keeping my uniform handy. I'm counting on being back next season. The guys finished second in the playoffs, but next year, when I'm back, I know we're gonna finish first.